WELCOME TO THE DATING GAME!

Meet some of New York's most eligible bachelors — each, in his own special way, the answer to that timeless question...

WHO IS PRINCE CHARMING?

IS HE:

    A. *Ellis Yuppington,* preppie entrepreneur who hungers for a "sensitive relationship" with a 5'8" Ivy League blonde?

    B. *Ernest Barnes,* cutthroat-but-cuddly lawyer who longs for a firm partnership?

    C. *Michael the Mime,* who seeks a sweet, loving wife to bear his children — if he can *afford* children?

    D. *Dr. David Hightest,* handsome and trendy psychoanalyst who was unfairly passed over — again — for Tycoon of the Year?

    E. *None of the above?*

AND NOW A WORD FROM OUR NARRATOR...

Allow me to introduce myself, girls — girls, ladies, women.... I am Prince Charming, your knight in shining armor. Your mother raised you on fairy tales based loosely on my adventures. You've been dreaming of me all your life. And when you reached twenty-five and were still unmarried, your mother insisted that I didn't exist.

But I love you. Wait for me. XXOO

COMPLICATIONS

PRINCE CHARMING

JOVE BOOKS, NEW YORK

This Jove book contains the complete
text of the original hardcover edition,
and was printed from new film.

COMPLICATIONS

A Jove Book / published by arrangement with
E. P. Dutton, a division of NAL Penguin Inc.

PRINTING HISTORY
E. P. Dutton edition published 1988
Published in Canada by Fitzhenry and Whiteside, Limited, Toronto
Jove edition / April 1990

ISBN: 0-515-10293-8

Jove Books are published by The Berkley Publishing Group,
200 Madison Avenue, New York, New York 10016.
The name "JOVE" and the "J" logo
are trademarks belonging to Jove Publications, Inc.

PRINTED IN THE UNITED STATES OF AMERICA

10 9 8 7 6 5 4 3 2 1

To the doctors who saved my life
and to Roy
who stuck around to see what I did with it.

Complications

Welcome to The City, girls—girls, women, ladies. I am Prince Charming, your knight in shining armor. I intend to be the most unobtrusive of narrators, so I wish to take the opportunity to thank you now. Without your support I wouldn't be where I am today.

Your mother raised you on fairy tales based loosely on my early adventures. You hoped for me, dreamt of me, and then, when you reached twenty-five and were still unmarried, your mother insisted that I didn't exist. Your faith in me has sometimes wavered. I understand. I understand you completely. And I love you. Wait for me. *XXOO.*

On this September morning, I bring you to a New York City apartment building in the East Sixties—Blackwatch Towers—a column of black glass that teases and flatters the sky. I would like you to meet three women, two of whom are still sleeping. Not one of them has your charm, but they each have a certain something.

Lizzie's hair is spread like spider lace across her pillow. She sleeps alone on a mattress on the floor. As soon as she wakes up, her face will tense with worry, and I may be forced to call her Elizabeth, but for now, Lizzie dreams sweetly—of me.

She does not know Marcy or Susan, though Susan and Marcy know each other, more or less.

Nobody is sleeping in Marcy's bed. Marcy is sleeping with Ernest, who has a place on Riverside Drive. She is dreaming about wild sex on a desert island, with Ernest. Marcy is faithful, even in her dreams, but her patience is limited. Ernest is dreaming about work. He is a lawyer. Last night they didn't make love. And they won't make love this morning. Maybe on the weekend. Maybe.

Susan has been awake since sunrise, and whatever she dreamt is swept safely out of her mind as she dictates into her micro-tape recorder.

"...and so I advise you, on behalf of Witkin, Pritkin and Harris, counsel for the defense, that we have determined your offer unsuitable for our client. Nonetheless we hope to reach a mutually agreeable settlement...."

Susan is the professional woman's professional woman. She and Ernest share an office and a secretary. They have for years. Professionally speaking, they're quite a team. Ernest doesn't know that Susan wears lace and silk underwear, and neither does anyone else. As Susan worked her way through Yale Law School, made Law Review, became a clerk at the Supreme Court, and made an impressive debut as an associate at Witkin, Pritkin & Harris, this didn't matter. There was always time. Love would come later. Now Susan is thirty-four, and she wears lace naughties to remind herself that she's a woman. We will keep this to ourselves, but occasionally Susan turns on the radio and dances in front of the mirror. But not now. She has work to do.

As she dictates, she clips her wavy chestnut hair into a tortoise-shell barrette. It's nearly seven; she'll have to finish on the way to work. She slides into her uniform: white silk blouse with a floppy paisley tie, and navy gabardine suit. She checks the suit in the mirror and slips off the skirt to banish an inappropriate crease with a deft swipe of the iron.

As Susan dashes out of Blackwatch Towers, she hands her laundry to the uniformed doorman, Julio.

"Susing," says Julio, "shirts are tomorrow."

Susan whips out her datebook. Julio is right.

"Damn."

"I'll take care of it. You stop running so hard. You listen to me."

"They don't make 'em like you anymore."

"The wimming alone needs a man to look after things."

Susan doesn't rebut his last argument. Julio has beckoned a cab. As the cab carries Susan down Second Avenue, he watches her move her lips against the black tape recorder she holds in her palm. Julio is a union member and a Latin, a Don Juan of the mind. He respectfully admires certain women tenants. He would never, ever, touch.

Ernest is going to be late. The superintendent in his building has turned off the water to work on the pipes. Ernest was too preoccupied to see the notice posted outside the elevator door last night, and now he can't shower, and he'll have to use the water that's left in the teakettle to shave.

Marcy hates to start a morning without a shower and a cup of life-giving coffee, so Ernest goes to elaborate pains not to wake her. He doesn't want to account for using coffee water to shave off his beard. Ernest never touches caffeine and doesn't understand his lover's passion for coffee. He just considers this one of Marcy's excesses; excess was what he loved about Marcy in the first place. Ernest is *excessively moderate.*

Being considerate, he decides not to kiss Marcy good-bye—he's on the way out and safe from her anticipated water crisis—because he doesn't want to wake her. This is a mistake. Marcy wakes up and not only is she no longer enjoying her sex-in-paradise dream, but she can't even make a damned cup of coffee in this damned apartment. For toppers, Ernest was too busy to manage a measly good-morning kiss. Why does she bother anymore?

As God made her, Marcy is a moderately attractive dishwater blonde. But over the past thirty-one years, Marcy has made considerable improvements on the good Lord's working draft, with all due respect. Marcy is striking. Her gift for shaping a whim into a trend has made her one of the hotter caterers in town—and she is on her way to becoming the hottest, thanks to raves in the *Times* and a profile in *Interview.* So why is Ernest's passion for work greater than his passion for her? She cancels the thought.

She's doing the Manstyle banquet at the Harvard Club on Wednesday. It has to be better than perfect. Yesterday, while Marcy was doing her tushy tucks, her assistant called to say she had met a tourist and fallen in love and would be going to Japan instead of going to work. The idea was so romantic Marcy could almost forgive her.

She dresses and drags herself over to a Broadway deli for a regular-to-go.

Lizzie hates to get out of bed on the morning of an audition. Forcing herself into a jittery vertical position, she mousses and fluffs her auburn curls. Everything is natural; the rusty color, the curls, the yellow-flecked gray eyes. Lizzie wonders if she'd be more successful as a blonde. On afternoons of unemployment between auditions and temporary secretarial jobs, Lizzie watches the soaps to remind herself that things could be worse. Lately they've been having the opposite effect. All the actresses on the soaps are blonde. All the actresses on the soaps are working. She is neither blonde nor working, which makes her a statistic. That, in itself, is comforting. It isn't her fault that only 2 percent of the actors in the city actually act for a living.

Last night, before descending into the subway, she stopped at a newsstand to buy something to read. What she read changed everything. It seemed that every major news and women's magazine was telling the same story. On the day Lizzie turned thirty, something she would do in eighty-nine days, she would become another statistic.

A word about these statistics: A recent study proves that 99.97 percent of all statistics are made up, and of those, 89 percent can be used to prove anything the statistician wants. Who concocts these statistics? Men! Not Prince Charming. Ordinary *Homo erections* who have a vested interest in your *not* waiting for me. If you ignore percentages and wait for me, with whom will the statisticians have affairs, children, imperfect lives? What have cold numbers to do with the sweet unaccountability of romantic anticipation? I trust you know that, despite suggestions to the contrary, someday, your prince *will* come. I remind you, you need only one. My Lizzie is a trifle more impressionable than you are.

She read that on her thirtieth birthday her chances of marrying the right man, *any* man, would be reduced to less than her odds of winning the New York State lottery. With that, the forces of Anxiety swooped down to carry her right over the edge.

Poor Lizzie. I am tempted to intervene, but it isn't someday yet.

The audition: The man doesn't speak, he quacks. She stands alone on a stage, suffering from light-blindness. Over the glaring barricade, director Chuck Canardino requests a bloodcurdling scream. Lizzie obliges.

5

"Okay. Now. Let me see you be strong and sexy and vulnerable and successful."

"All at once?"

"Of course, baby. You're a woman of the eighties."

She does her best. There is a long, loud silence. Finally, Ann Hedonia, Canardino's casting agent, says those immortal words:

"Next, please."

"I can go blonde, too, if that's better for the part," offers Lizzie. No response. The hell with this, Lizzie thinks. And before she strides offstage, she clearly and distinctly sticks out her tongue.

Status Quo

On her lunch hour, Susan wanders over to Brooks Brothers. She has a vague yearning for something new, but she's looking for it in the same old places.

The Madison Avenue entrance is blocked. The U.S. mission is hosting a goodwill tour for new Third World delegates to the United Nations, and Brooks Brothers is a must-see. Susan recognizes the need for international understanding and cooperation, so she stands aside as a stream of turbaned and robed and caftaned and pantalooned and kilted men enter this bastion of neutrality. When the last batik has disappeared through the single glass door, she enters, and instantly feels drowsy.

The clerk means to be helpful. Susan wants to add some sartorial zip. Having only the deliberately unchic contents of Brooks Brothers' Professional Women's Department at his disposal, the clerk brings Susan a red skirt and a yellow shirt from the Corporate Wives Section on the far right side of the floor.

Susan passes half her lunch hour deliberating in front of a dressing room mirror. She studies herself from all angles, adjusts, readjusts, but this country club look is all wrong. This isn't what she had in mind, not at all.

"I can't do it," she calls from behind the curtain.

"It's being done," the clerk reassures her.

"It may be being done, but it's certainly not the done thing at W, P and H."

"The color is very flattering."

"Do you have anything sexy?" The clerk stiffens at the mention of the s-word. Susan is embarrassed. "Never mind. I'll take a half dozen of those regimental stripe floppy ties."

Neither Susan nor the clerk is satisfied, but they've made it through a crisis and the status quo is maintained.

You're Not Half the Man
You Used to Be
and You Never Were

The sad fact is, certain women, finding themselves drawn to the deceptively alluring traits of a man with dubious intentions, are apt, in their eagerness to experience True Love, to mistake such a man for me—often with uncomfortable results. Once a damsel has made this mistake she is more than likely to make it again. If she does this often enough, when she meets me, what happens? She sees right through me and my white steed with the golden mane because she no longer believes I exist. Pity.

Lizzie's mistake, Ellis Yuppington, is a prematurely rich thirty-year-old entrepreneur who believes that he can have it all, all at once. He is, at this moment, making unorthodox use of a taxicab with a woman who is not Lizzie.

Lizzie doesn't know she's made a mistake. She waits for Ellis, past the hour of their appointment, in a crowded SoHo bistro frequented by the trendoisie. The maître d' has taken a shine to her. He brings her one seltzer water while she waits, and then one more as she continues to wait.

"You are waiting for someone very special?"

"I think he is. Yes."

"He should know better than to permit a beautiful woman to wait," says the maître d' as he glides away.

Lizzie sneaks a look at herself in the window. For a poverty-stricken old maid failure teetering on the brink of a lifetime of solitude and loneliness, I'm not too bad, she reflects.

Lizzie doesn't see Ellis embrace the woman who has been sharing his cab and what is known in the trade as his throbbing member, but coincidentally she turns around and sees Ellis blowing a kiss. She assumes it is for her and she smiles.

"Lizzie! Lizzie! We've got to talk."

"I've been all ears for an hour already, Ellis."

Ellis takes her hand and kisses it. Then he kisses her wrist and the inside of her elbow. "I've kept you waiting."

"Oh, that's okay."

"Sweet one," he whispers, "listen. I've been thinking about the two of us."

Lizzie curls a strand of hair prettily around her finger.

"We've been together, what? Two and a half months, and you've kind of become my best friend..."

Lizzie takes his hand and answers lovingly, "I know. I feel the same way."

"...but it's not what I want. Not exactly."

Lizzie feels her hand turn cold and numb. "Did I do something? What is it you want?"

"I want us to stay friends, but..."

The maître d' swoops over the table to personally deliver their drinks. "I love love, don't you," he gushes. Ellis and Lizzie muster polite upward curvatures of the mouth and wait silently for the maître d' to leave.

"I see myself with someone else," says Ellis at the earliest possible opportunity.

"Who?"

Ellis considers carefully before answering. He doesn't see himself with his taxicab lover, not really. Finally he blurts out the truth. "I haven't met her yet, but I can tell you some things about her. She's upscale. A successful blonde. About five ten. She's gone to a Swiss boarding school for girls, all girls, and finished at an Ivy League college. She adores Northern Renaissance art. You—well, I like you. I may even love you, but—"

"I'm a downscale, out-of-work actress."

"Oh, Lizzie. I don't want to hurt you. I'm just trying to be honest."

"Just today I was thinking about blonde. This sheds a whole new light."

"Oh, Lizzie."

"I'm five ten!"

"I love that about you," Ellis says tenderly.

Lizzie pries her dead hand out of Ellis's. "Would you excuse me for just a moment?" she says as she stands.

Lizzie heads for the ladies' room to have a bawl, but on the way over she changes her mind and beckons the maître d'.

He hurries to her side. "So you were not disappointed?"

"Oh, no," Lizzie whispers confidentially. "In fact, we have something important to celebrate. I'd appreciate it enormously if you'd take care of a round of drinks for everyone in the restaurant, and place it on our tab."

"He's a lucky man," says the maître d'.

* * *

Ellis is savoring his drink when Lizzie returns to the table.

"So," says Lizzie, "we were on your trying to be honest."

"Don't be angry."

"Why should I be angry?"

Ellis takes this at face value and is pleased that he has gracefully handled what might have been a delicate maneuver. Men, women, at the bar and the scattered tables, seem to be noticing him, raising their glasses in his direction. He nods. All told, he figures, he deserves these congratulatory toasts. He assumes they must have seen the article about his latest business conquest in *Venture* magazine.

"Lizzie, you've helped me to become a more sensitive person," he offers. "That's a real plus in your favor. But I suspect that you're looking for a commitment."

Lizzie is looking around the room. "Why would I be looking for a commitment?"

"I'm just trying..."

"...to be honest." Lizzie only finishes sentences when she knows exactly how they will end. "Ellis," she says, "I have had about all the sensitivity I can take today, okay? I hope you and your imagination will be blissfully happy together."

Lizzie winks as she passes the maître d' on her way out the door. Under the circumstances, she's happy. She said what she would have wanted to say and did what she would have fantasized about doing. The maître d' is happy.

Ellis is merely content. The denouement was a little rockier than he normally likes. Everything can't go smoothly all the time, he reasons. He is pleasantly distracted by a new rash of customers raising their glasses in his direction. He accepts their toasts. The maître d' presents the check for seventy-four drinks, face-down.

"Thank you very much," he says.

"Thank *you*," Ellis oozes. He likes this place. They recognize him. He holds a bit of whiskey in his mouth and enjoys the warmth. He's in no hurry, so he leaves the check untouched and leans back in his chair.

Susan Gives Marcy Advice
Which Will Have
Unforeseen Consequences

The Witkin, Pritkin & Harris hiring process is abominably slow when it comes to support staff. Ernest and Susan are forced to hire a temporary secretary while they wait for Personnel to wake from a hundred-year slumber.

Their current temp, a nineteen-year-old cosmetic queen, thinks a legal brief is something a lawyer wears under his pants.

"There are no men," she declares as she balances the phone between her chin and her shoulder. "I mean there are men but there aren't any real men. Male men. Real males." The phone rings. "Hold please."

"W, P and H . . . Oh, hi. Nothing. Yes. I'd absolutely love to. Hold a sec."

Susan saunters into the reception area. She is wondering why the client didn't return her call. "Anything for me?"

The cosmetic queen rubs two lined and glossed lips together and blots. "It's been absolutely dead." The phone rings. "W, P and H." Susan hovers. "Oh, hi. Yes, I'd absolutely adore to. Can you hang on?"

Susan retreats to her office, but leaves the door open because she'd hate to miss the show. As would I. This kind of woman has no use for Prince Charming. She is born with an egalitarian blindness that eliminates the need to choose one functioning male over another. The secretary puts party three on hold and returns to party one. "Honey, I'll have to get back to you. It's *him* on the other line." She disconnects party one and picks up on line two. "Darling, they persecute me. I'm absolutement swamped around here. I'll have to get back to you." She returns to party three who has been promoted to party one and cups her hand over the receiver. No one can hear what she whispers next.

Susan suddenly wants to get moving. She's impatient now, irritated as she watches the cosmetic queen slouch sensuously in her chair. Back to work.

She knocks on Ernest's office door. "Ern? Let's go."

Ernest is tossing crumpled attempts at a draft of his opening argument into the wastebasket across the room. It helps him think.

"Enter."

Ernest at thirty-three is no glittering Adonis. He's cuddlier than he is sexy. Just this moment Susan has a very inappropriate fantasy. She imagines herself curling up on his lap, giving him a little nuzzle. What's wrong with her today? She's on the verge.

Instead, she says, "You don't look particularly ready to roll."

"Honoroff is sitting in on the trial. I want to be brilliant."

Honoroff is *the* senior partner at W, P & H. Ernest and Susan are eligible to become partners in the firm. If there is one man to impress, it's Honoroff.

"We'll be brilliant. Dazzle, dazzle."

Ernie cracks a grin. "This is it. It's time to fish or cut throat, and you're madame confident."

"Cut bait."

"We don't make partner and I'll cut throat, thank you very much. We're talking about success here, the big S."

"Well, I'm not so sure the big S is worth the price I paid for it."

Ernie has no answer for this, and no idea why Susan is being so cranky.

Marcy is having a mega-crisis because she has exhausted all her known resources without finding a replacement for the assistant who was stolen from her by love. You'd think there were lots of assistants in Manhattan, but where are they when you need them?

She finds herself in Midtown, and dashes in to see Ernie. Maybe he can help. At least he can comfort her.

"Oh, Ern, I'm having a mega-crisis," she exclaims as she crumples dramatically into his arms. Ern is slightly pleased and slightly embarrassed.

"Hi, Marce," says Susan.

"We're just on the way out," says Ernest.

"My assistant has fallen passionately in love with a Japanese tourist who is whisking her away to Kyoto two days before the Manstyle banquet."

"I don't think Japanese men are very cute," says the cosmetic queen.

Marcy bursts into tears.

"That just doesn't happen," Ernie decides.

"They fell in love. He plays infield for the Kyoto Animalues."

"That is a problem," Susan observes. "So. You need someone to help you with the Manstyle banquet to honor the fifty most eligible, successful, and desirable recipients of the Manstyle men-of-the-year awards? At the Harvard

Club?" Susan puts down her briefcase. "Sorry, Ern, you'll have to go to court alone. I volunteer."

"That's not funny," snuffles Marcy. Even Marcy never thinks of Susan as a woman with an eye for men.

"We've got to get moving or we'll be late," says Ernest. "I'm sorry, sweetheart, I'm just a bit preoccupied." Ernie draws Marcy into his arms and strokes her hair. She is not comforted.

The three of them step into the elevator.

"I need help. I'm serious."

"Okay. We'll talk about it later." Ernest consoles her with a peck.

Ernest has just crossed into no-man's-land. "Later will be too late." Ernest feels a chill in Marcy's tone that promises trouble when later gets around to being now.

They ride the rest of the way to the ground floor in silence. As they step out onto the sidewalk, Susan says, "Marce, have you thought of calling a temporary agency? Try Busy Bee. That's the one we use."

"For this?"

"Why not? You're the brains. All you need is a warm body."

"I certainly do," Marcy drawls. "Thank you, Susan. You're so helpful and thoughtful and considerate and caring—"

"Message received. Over and out," says Ernie, as he prays for a taxi to materialize and whisk him away from feminine rage. His wish is granted. Ernest wants to give Marcy what she wants, but he's never quite sure what that is. He knows he hasn't come up with it yet. He thinks about playing racquetball after the trial. Racquetball he understands. There are rules. You can win.

Mud: The Great Equalizer

Marcy calls Busy Bee. A woman answers. "Busy Bee. A Busy Bee is a happy bee." Marcy almost hangs up.

"How do you know a busy bee is a happy bee?"

"We just assume they're happy. How may we help you?"

"Is this a honey farm or temp agency?" Marcy whines. She's been through too much. She wonders if her credit card balance will withstand a binge at Henri Bendel's.

Marcy's mood sweetens when the beekeeper on the line assures her she will have an assistant meet her at the Chi-chi Charcuterie at 8:30 the next morning. Marcy decides she can forgo the Bendel's binge and settle for a facial.

Lizzie has been sloshing through the muck of life all day and has finally received what might be considered, considering the rest of her luck, some good news. Busy Bee temps called and asked if she'd like to do some catering and prep work on the Manstyle banquet. She got into temp work so she wouldn't have to wait tables because nothing was more boring than an actress waiting tables. But then, Lizzie was beginning to doubt that she was an actress. She hadn't had a part since she played the Froot Loops Toucan. She doesn't see the point in having pride at the moment since the money is exceptional.

She decides she yearns for a facial, a good facial at a ridiculously expensive salon. She's never had one. She can't afford it. That's why she needs it. She goes to the instant money dispenser:

> HELLO. WELCOME TO THE MONEYBANK USER FRIENDLY CASH MACHINE. HOW ARE YOU TODAY? I'M NOT SO BAD MYSELF THOUGH MY CIRCUITS ARE KILLING ME AND SOME IDIOT TRIED TO JAM AN UPSIDE DOWN CARD IN MY SLOT. ANYWAY, WHAT WAS IT YOU WANTED?

That's the limit. She wishes the banks would go back to using rude tellers. Lizzie considers stuffing her money in a mattress. She has so little money, she'd be better off using a sock. She heads straight for Elizabeth Arden where she will be pampered and tended and soothed.

Franzl von Hapsburg will see to it. Franzl von Hapsburg was born Howard Splotstein forty years ago in the Bronx. During his stint in the army he mastered German and returned to the States with an accent and the cachet that comes from being a handsome, foreign homosexual. He clubs with the Eurotrash by night and makes mud masques and vegetable compresses for women who relax at the touch of his fingers by day. Franzl sometimes thinks it a pity that his admiration for feminine beauty is purely professional.

"Franzie, I love you," Marcy murmurs from under a hardening clay paste. Franzl places cucumbers over her eyes.

"You are a princess, liebling."

"I wish Ernie thought so."

"Liebling, you must forget Ernie. He is bad for your

complexion. You need..." Lizzie enters Franzl's cubicle holding her pink cotton Elizabeth Arden robe closed at the neck. "Ach! Excuse me, liebling. Think beautiful thoughts. Think closed pores."

"Closed pores," murmurs Marcy.

Franzl loves to introduce the uninitiated to the sensual delight of a good facial treatment. This pretty redhead is so tense that her cheek muscles practically vibrate. He rubs Lizzie's face, crooning, "Relax. Peace. Tranquility. Cool sparkling lake. Now waterfalls. Now the birds are singing and a wind caresses you. Relax." He mixes a bowl of pink goop and slathers it across her features. "Now I am covering you with a tingling kiss. You relax and you are in a forest. You see Bambi."

Lizzie is so relaxed that tears have begun to trickle down her face.

"Ach! Liebling! No tears. Zey vill dilute your masque. Ze masque is essential to ze face of ze beautiful woman. I vill make you beautiful, irresistible, beautiful. Now...where were we?"

"Bambi," Lizzie offers helpfully.

"Now, as I cover your eyes, think you are Sleeping Beauty at rest in a beautiful castle." Franzie slaps two cukes over Lizzie's eyes, and retreats to the back room to smoke a weed.

"All these broads got problems," he mutters to himself.

Therapy

Everybody's got problems, or I would not be telling you this story. Were it not for problems, no one would dream of salvation. If no one dreamt of salvation, Prince Charming would be a legend only in my mind. And we wouldn't want that.

You may think me wildly sympathetic to women. That is one of my charms. But I see in every man a glimmer of myself. As for the ones who behave badly: One woman I rescued offered the unscientific theory that when a baby boy is circumcised, the nerve endings joining the body and the emotions are severed. That may be what certain parties wish unsuspecting damsels to believe. Lowers those nagging expectations. Of course, the theory's as much nonsense as the notion of a balanced national budget, as any honest man with or without a prepuce will tell you.

Both Ellis Yuppington and Dr. David Hightest are circumcised, but that has nothing to do with their emotional states. It is more pertinent to note that both men are functioning and active.

Dr. David Hightest is Ellis Yuppington's psychiatrist. Hightest knows nearly everything about Yuppington. Yuppington knows virtually nothing about Hightest. This arrangement suits them both.

While Susan stands in court with Ernest, and Marcy and Lizzie sit side by side caked with mud (but not yet having met), Ellis reclines on a Freudian leather couch and David stares out the window.

David should be listening to his patient, but privation has driven him to dwell on something more compelling. Despite partially inherited tycoonish wealth, all the charm money can buy, the elongated features, sandy hair, and ship-stern jaw of a Ralph Lauren model, what some might call brilliance, and a full-time, but discreet publicist, David Hightest was again overlooked by *Manstyle* magazine. He will not be receiving one of the fifty Most Eligible Tycoon awards. He has been holding a place on the wall for that award since he finished his residency. What does it take to have what it takes?

"Mmm," he murmurs, to cover his drifting attention. He knows what Ellis has been talking about. They've been going over this topic for weeks. "Have you considered that maybe you have all these standards so that you really don't have to become emotionally involved with any one woman?"

"Maybe," Ellis concedes. "But I would get involved with the right woman, if I met her. It's just, well, it's hard to find someone who meets my needs."

"Needs?" Sometimes David thinks a computer could do his job.

"Culture, beauty, no shorter than five nine, blonde, though I'd be willing to compromise on the hair, wealth, good muscle tone, but not too good, ability to beat me at tennis. And art. She must have a powerful interest in Northern Renaissance art."

David chews on this last remark. The rest he can well

understand. "You've never mentioned an interest in Northern Renaissance art."

"I don't have one. That's why the right woman has to. Balance out the gene pool."

That explains everything. David jots down a note to remind himself to ask Ellis what else he feels he is lacking. David feels a glimmer of empathy for his patient, but the fifty-minute hour is over.

"I'm sorry. We'll have to stop now."

With all due respect for the concept that time is money, Ellis stops instantly. At Hightest's prices, his emotions can wait a week.

A Miss Is as Good
as a Mile

    The Hall of Records, which houses Surrogates
Court, truly resembles a temple of justice. My dear
friend, the goddess Athena, is particularly fond of this
Chambers Street monument. It makes her long nostal-
gically for her own days on the bench. I don't have much
of an interest in courtroom drama. The romance business
makes its own laws. You will please excuse me, therefore,
if I do not detail the case in which Ernest and Susan have
just been victorious. From my point of view, the important thing is this:

    When the verdict is announced, Honoroff gives a
nod of absolute and significant approval to the young
lawyers. The victory with Honoroff is worth as much to
them as the victory for the client. They shake hands with
the client. Ernest claps the client on the back as the courtroom empties.

    Left alone with his colleague after a day of restraint
and polished argument, Ernest indulges in an all-out
grin. He loosens his red power tie and his courtroom de-
corum, throwing his arms around Susan so vigorously

that she loses her balance. She timidly places her two arms around his waist, almost getting up the nerve to hold him tighter. But then the hug is over.

Susan tries to relive the sensation she felt at Ernest's embrace as she walks north toward SoHo. She has to walk. She wants to feel her body, release the energy that has been pressing against her ribs for weeks. She finds herself in the marble and steel boutique, Les Filles de la Rue des Femmes de Paris au New York II. Under the influence of a remaining tingle, she buys herself a body-hugging seashell pink angora sweater with a scoop neck that teases the top of her décolletage, *and* she wears it out of the store.

The rewards are ample. As she strolls up Broome Street, enjoying the once-over of the masculine passersby, her tingle is enhanced by a certain guilty pleasure. Susan is not behaving like the woman she thinks she is. As her stroll takes her through the gay neighborhood of Christopher Street in Greenwich Village, attention dwindles. Susan hails a cab, and heads for the Elizabeth Arden salon. As she steps out onto upper Fifth Avenue, she puts her jacket back on. She is in an area where someone she knows might see her.

Marcy and Lizzie won't meet until tomorrow, but they have both finished their facial treatments and returned separately to Blackwatch Towers by the time Susan settles under Franzl von Hapsburg's delicate touch. She closes her eyes and submits to Franzl's caresses as her imagination wanders down the rest of her body.

Warning:
Sexual Content

Little of the legendary material about Prince Charming has dealt directly with my sexual ability. When you first learned of my existence, sex was as much of an abstraction as I have sometimes seemed to be.

The stirring of sexual feelings in my dear Susan may augur a turn in her story, not to mention the stories of Lizzie and Marcy. We may feel safe in assuming that at one point or another in the near future these feelings will be expressed outside of the imagination, may we not? For this reason, I shall be the slightest bit indelicate. My love for you necessitates that I speak frankly.

I, Prince Charming, anticipate your every desire before you speak it. I live to love you, and wise is the damsel who waits for my true love. In all modesty I must tell you that I alone will climb with you to heights of passion you have not dared to dream of. I know where to stroke you, to kiss you, without a gesture or word of instruction. I know when to slow down, and when to race forward. I know how roughly or gently you want to be held. And I know Romance. Trust that I will always know when you want to hear me say I love you, want you, need you only. Our love will last forever. *Forever.*

Try to say as much for the subspecies *Homo erection.* Mere men may try, and try their best, but Prince Charming is Prince Charming for a reason, my darlings.

I will, of course, forgive you if you do not wait for me. You must remember that I understand the real you completely, and I wouldn't change a thing. I don't want you to be hurt or disappointed in love, so I urge you to remember this: The mere man to whom you give your heart will not know what you are thinking—unless you tell him. He will not instinctively know how to please you. You may have to show him. And lastly, my fairest ones, he may not say the things you long to hear exactly when you most long to hear them. If you accept these three limitations, you may be able to live contentedly without me.

Oh my beloved, the thought bathes me with sorrow. I urge you once again to wait for me and a life of sublime happiness together ever after.

Julio Keeps Track

Julio the doorman lives in a respectable Dominican section of Spanish Harlem. He is a family man with one son and five daughters, all virgins. Half his fascination with the job at Blackwatch Towers has to do with watching these downtown (for him) uptown (for them) women conduct their lives. He often wonders where their fathers are. If he caught Maria, Sophia, Angela, Rosita, or Marie-Gracia running around like these American women (God forbid and Holy Mother forgive him), he would murder them, plain and simple. A man cannot tolerate such disgrace. When Julio found a copy of *Sex and the Sensuous Senorita* under Angela's pillow, she was grounded for a week. Later that night, after his wife was asleep, he undertook the fatherly duty of reading *Sex and the Sensuous Senorita* himself, from cover to cover. A man must be aware of the influences on his daughters.

He thanks the Virgin that he is not the father of all the daughters in this building. A man looks at women who are not his daughters with a different kind of pleasure. Julio rarely tells his wife of the goings-on in the building. A man does not want his wife, and the mother of his daughters, to know such things.

Although he doubts the virginity of Marcy, Lizzie, and even Susan, they are relatively "good" girls, in his eyes. Now they are all safely at home and Julio's shift is almost over.

Lizzie has gone to sleep. She'd just as soon the day be over. Tomorrow, she'll keep as busy as she can. She doesn't want to have time to feel.

Marcy is making lists. Lists of groceries she needs to buy for the Manstyle do, and lists of the pros and cons of her relationship with Ernest. On the pro side, Ernest is stable, hardworking and financially secure, reasonably good-looking, kind, and in love with her. Every Wednesday he brings her a bouquet of flowers which he selects himself. On the con side, Ernest is so stable, so hardworking that their sex life is a snooze. He is only reasonably good-looking, not the drop-dead gorgeous mega-man she dreams of. He is kind but often preoccupied, and so boringly in love with her that she wonders whether he would notice if she wasn't around for the event. Every damned week he gets her flowers, always flowers, never flaming hot red split-crotch panties to be worn during sex grabbed spontaneously in inappropriate places. Not a chance. Not ever. Beside this, her grocery list pales.

Susan is feeling pretty. Her face is still flushed from the facial. In the privacy of her apartment, she can admire the fit of the pink sweater. There is one other thing. On the way home Susan bought a hair-painting kit. If she works up the courage, she will add some blonde highlights to her already beautiful chestnut hair. She has carefully read the instructions, clipped a small strand of hair, and placed it in a small dish of hair-painting solution. The entire apartment smells of ammonia.

Her briefcase waits for her on the overstuffed velvet couch. There's the reality, she thinks. Susan turns on the classical music station and settles in for a night of the usual.

Julio smiles with recognition as Ernest enters the lobby holding a bouquet of tulips.

"Good evening."

"Good evening, Julio, I'm here to see..."

"...Miss Lightner?"

It's an honest mistake.

"I'll look in on Marcy later, but don't buzz up. Wednesday's her usual flower night, but she's busy this Wednesday, so I thought I'd surprise her."

"I'm sure Miss Lightner will be delighted," Julio comments approvingly. Ernest is a worthy man. A good man. It's a pity he isn't Spanish.

"I'd appreciate it if you'd let Miss Susan Whitbread know I was here."

Without comment, Julio turns to the intercom. Even a nice man like Ernest cannot be trusted, he thinks, but he smiles. This is not his world.

Susan isn't expecting company, and so, when the intercom buzzes, she pitches a manila folder into the air. When she learns who has come to see her, she pitches herself into a minor frenzy. Should she change out of her sexy sweater? No. But she does. As she shimmies into a broadcloth button-down shirt, she grabs a can of room deodorizer.

There is a closed bottle of expensive wine on the counter. Susan quickly uncorks it and takes a swig. Not wanting Ernest to think she's just opened a new bottle of wine, she pours a few ounces down the drain and sticks the bottle behind the decomposing Brie in the refrigerator.

The doorbell rings.

Susan checks herself in the mirror and takes the plunge.

"Hi, Ern. This is a surprise." She notices the varicolored tulips immediately. Can he really be bringing her a bouquet at home after work on a day that is months from her birthday?

"I hope I'm not messing up your evening...." Ernest doesn't hand the bouquet to Susan. It would not cross his mind to think for a moment that it might cross Susan's mind to think that the bouquet is for her.

"No problem," says Susan, sauntering over to the refrigerator. "I think I have a little wine left over."

Ernest admires a stunning tapestry which hangs on Susan's wall. "What is this?" he asks as he accepts the glass Susan offers.

"That represents my best investment."

"It's from the Middle Ages or something, isn't it?"

"Close." Susan tries a flirtatious look, but she isn't sure how it comes across. Her flirtation muscles have atrophied. "Renaissance, really. From Belgium."

Ernest nods appreciatively.

"You here to celebrate our stunning victory?" Susan gestures in the direction of the flowers.

Ernie is flustered. He holds out the bouquet to Susan. "Well. A little celebration is in order. But actually, after my racquetball game, I realized you had the Burleigh file. I was on my way home, so I thought I'd stop over and pick it up."

"Of course," chokes Susan.

"You're a champ, Suze." Ernest raises his glass in a toast.

Their glasses meet in the air. "Thanks. Thanks for the flowers, too, Ern. That was sweet."

Ernie glances at his watch. "Marce has got this big

thing on Wednesday and I probably won't get to see her. Do you think she'd still be up now?"

Susan gestures to her phone. As Ernie dials, Susan sneaks a look at the hair clipping bathing in its stinking paint. She can't distinguish the hair from the dish it is sitting in. It's been soaking too long; all the color has been bleached out.

The Blow

Marcy doesn't miss the flowers because it isn't Wednesday. She doesn't miss them until Ernest explains.

"So what could I do? She was so delighted I just couldn't tell her," he laughs, as he nuzzles Marcy's neck.

Then Marcy thinks Ernest is incapable of doing anything right. Ernest would have to be wearing a fur serape not to sense the chill in the room; the storm is coming but he can't tell from which side. He feels like he's just eaten a bowl of lead pudding.

"So!" he says, affecting good cheer.

"So what?" mutters his beloved. "So why mention it at all?"

Ernest loosens his tie. After a day in court and two hours on the courts, he is not interested in another test of his strength.

"I know you're under a lot of pressure, Marce. But I have some good news."

"That's wonderful," she says absently, plunking herself on the couch. Ernest snuggles beside her. Marcy smiles before she can stop herself. "So tell me some good news. How did it go?"

"We won. But more than that." Ernest attempts a dramatic pause. Marcy picks at her fingernail polish.

"Well what for chrissake?"

"I don't want to tell you if you're going to be cranky."

"Look. I've got a lot of stuff to do tonight, Ern. I really want to know but not if it's going to take me seven hours to find out."

Marcy walks to her desk and turns the list detailing Ernest's faults face-down. Then, struck with an unanticipated bolt of guilt, she cuddles on Ernest's knee. "Oooh, how romantic!" Ernie croons with more than a few trace elements of sarcasm in his voice.

Marcy kisses the top of Ernest's head, noticing that his hair seems thinner than it was two years ago. "I'm sorry, sweetling. Let's start over."

"That's my girl. We've both had a long day."

Ernest is always kind, thinks Marcy. She kisses his lips. He responds with more strength than usual, pressing hard against her. She takes off his tie. He looks at her coyly and then grabs her and tosses her down on the couch. "I'm pouncing on you," he says. He's just as surprised as she is.

"I see that."

Ernest slips Marcy's blouse over her head. Marcy hastily unbuttons Ernest's shirt. As she rubs her breasts against the soft hair on Ernest's chest, she reaches to unzip, unbutton, and unhook Ernest's sex-proof Brooks Brothers trousers to get at the hardness underneath. By the time her hand slides freely, what she was reaching for is gone. Ernie looks upset.

"Don't worry, sweetling. I'll take care of the both of you."

Ernie looks even more upset.

"It's just . . . well . . . I'm feeling a little preoccupied."

The instant desire killer. She might as well be caressing a trout, she thinks as she extracts her hand and pulls her blouse around her shoulders.

Ernie tries to lure Marcy back to his side. "Marce. Honoroff said he'd put me in for partner today. Me and Suze."

"That's great, Ern. Terrifico," says Marcy at 98.4 degrees.

"Of course they still have to approve it. Nothing's certain until it's official."

"Looks good for you, Ern." Marcy is now at 50 Fahrenheit.

"Want to hear how the case went?"

"I wanted," Marcy drawls, "to make love." Jack Frost is nipping at her nose.

"We will," says Ernest soothingly. "It's just this moment I—"

"It has been almost a year now of your putting me off or putting me on hold. I'm frustrated, Ernest. You know what I mean, Ernest? A la dying on the vine."

"I love you," the well-meaning Ernest offers.

"Not the way I need to be loved, Ern. You put all your sex in your work. I need a man who puts his sex in me."

I cringe along with him. He is no Prince Charming; he lacks fizz. But he is a good man, if not always a hard man.

Ernest tries to take Marcy into his arms, to make love to her now. Marcy pulls away.

"I'm sorry, Ern. I have work to do."

I will tell you what I know. Ernest wanted to make partner before he proposed marriage to Marcy. This is half of why he has been working so damnably hard, and why he is often so tired. He was waiting for the right moment to tell her of his plans.

Mistake. The right moment is never later. Almost never, at any rate. Prince Charming would have known that he should nurture your love all along, never keeping that precious love waiting, never permitting the pursuit of daily bread and outrageous fortune to interfere with the most important thing: you.

Unfortunately, the wrong moment beat the right one to the finish line. This is my point. Wait for me, and you will not be disappointed.

Ernest stumbles out of the apartment. As he leaves Blackwatch Towers, he trips over a sleeping bum. "Why don't you watch where you're going," Ernest mutters to the bum.

The bum could pull a knife, but for all his years on the street, he has never hit a man worse off than himself. He sleeps in only the best doorways, which usually allows for a lot of leeway. He leaves the hardship case in the suit alone.

Marcy is too upset to work so she crawls into bed with a Harlequin novel that never disappoints her, *Flames of Desire*. Ernest has never known that Marcy reads Harlequins. Marcy has never known that Ernest has had a glance or two at a Harlequin himself. He thought it would help him to understand what women wanted, what Marcy wanted.

Alas.

A Loss,
but Not a Lack

Ernest takes the day off. He buys himself a leather jacket and a pair of Marithe & Francois Girbaud destroyed blue jeans, his first pair of jeans since law school. He buys himself two handwoven Italian sports shirts at Charivari. Then he buys himself a Missoni sweater. He buys himself a pair of chocolate suede Belgian loafers. He buys himself a VCR. He buys himself a membership to Jack La Lanne.

He orders lunch at Le Cirque. Then he feels better. Almost like a new man. He would like to be a new man. When his demi-filet of blush veal *avec* slivers *des amandes et pâle bleu oignons sur riz de Camargue* and his asparagus tips in apricot sauce arrive, he digs in without blanching, but there is just so much newness a man can tolerate in one day. When the check arrives, Ernest wonders if there is another route to *nouveau savoir-vivre* that is maybe just a little less steep.

Still, he has the right idea. As my fairy godmother used to say, a change is as good as a rest.

Marcy Meets Lizzie

Marcy would like to say that she has swept Ernest entirely from her mind, but she has not. As one of your contemporary soothsayers, a Mr. Neil Sedaka, used to sing, breaking up is a pain in the tail feathers.

Marcy is, however, blessed with a mighty preoccupation. As she stands outside the Chi-chi Charcuterie, she prays that her Busy Bee temp will arrive as scheduled. And her wish is granted.

Lizzie consults a piece of paper for the correct address and congratulates herself. She has an unerring sense of direction. She notices a frosted blonde wearing six silver strands of beads and silver shoes at either end of an all-black outfit. As there is no one else on the street, she deduces that this must be the caterer.

Similarly, Marcy evaluates the redhead. Is that natural color? She can't tell. Either that, or a damned good dye job, and why would a woman who could afford that be on the street in front of the Chi-chi Charcuterie at 8:27 A.M.?

"Are you the Busy Bee temp?" she ventures.

"I'm Lizzie. And you are?"

"Marcy."

This is a significant moment, my darlings. You must trust me on that point.

Marcy examines her temporary assistant. "Well," she declares, "you look normal enough. You don't plan to fall in love within the next twenty-four hours, do you?"

Lizzie, who sometimes thinks she's heard it all, hasn't heard this one before. "This *is* a catering job, isn't it?" she responds.

And they're off.

The Chi-chi Charcuterie dangles all manner of mammals trussed and hung by their hind feet in the window. When Julia Child is at home in Cambridge, she shops at Savenors. In New York, if she is prevailed upon to cook, she shops here. The Charcuterie stocks rhinoceros and rattlesnake steak. If you know the butcher, you can occasionally get your paws on lion loin.

"We'll need forty pounds of ground round to the Harvard Club by five-thirty," says Marcy. This casual remark sets a trend and creates a small scandal that will reverberate across the meat world for days.

"Ground round!" the butcher utters.

"*Le menu est nouvel américain,*" Marcy assures him.

He nods. Marcy knows what Ernest cannot even guess. Nouvelle French cuisine is as out as black clothing will be two seasons from now. America is in. We are all bullish on America, the America that helps build strong bodies twelve ways and fights terrorism.

Marcy orders two hundred Wonder Bread hamburger buns and a case of Hellmann's Real All-American Mayonnaise. She and Lizzie ride out to Yankee Stadium and buy gee-whiz yellow Squirt-Em-Good canisters of AAA-1 Gulden's mustard.

It is difficult to find the toothpicks Marcy knows she needs, so she goes to Queens, where you can find everything in stock. A small souvenir shop under the shadow of the 1964 World's Fair Globe produces the desired plastic bathing beauties writhing on toothpicks.

"How post-feminist!" Lizzie exclaims.

This girl *understands,* thinks Marcy. They return to Manhattan with the vital elements in the back of Marcy's van. There is only one more stop. They pull up in front of an elegant townhouse on East Thirty-eighth Street. There is no address on the building, no sign of what is inside. It is an unmarked chocolaterie, known only to the cutting edge of the New York cognoscenti. Marcy enters with confidence, leading an awestruck Lizzie behind her.

They leave with $5,862.39 worth of chocolate. Lizzie cannot help but remark that they have just spent more on chocolate than she earned in the first third of the year.

"But it's worth it," says Marcy surveying the chocolate-covered strawberries, chocolate-covered pretzels, fifty Devonshire cream—filled chocolate Statues of Liberty with golden flames, white-chocolate-covered popcorn, rose petals with chocolate edges, bittersweet-chocolate-covered grasshoppers, chocolate-covered flies with fresh fruit jelly eyes, and a special custom order of rum-chocolate-covered army ants.

We are all familiar with the research which indicates that after eating chocolate the body simulates the sensation of euphoria associated with being in love. En route to the Harvard Club, Marcy drives past Ernie's office building ("That's where Ernie works") and then takes a detour past Ernie's Riverside Drive apartment ("That's Ernie's place").

"Who's Ernie, anyway?" asks Lizzie, as any reasonable person would.

Marcy sighs. "The sweetest, most generous, stable man I know. Did I say responsible? He's responsible, too."

"Sounds perfect to me," Lizzie reasons.

Marcy tenders a slightly rude-sounding snort.

Manstyle

      Put aside all thoughts of love derailed. Think of this: Marcy and Lizzie, with the aid of several brawny workers, are turning the hallowed recesses of the Harvard Club into a hometown picnic.

      Lizzie carries a Styrofoam chestnut tree to the corner of the banquet hall. Marcy attends to the finer points, laying her precious rum-chocolate army ants across the plaid tablecloths for which she had scoured thrift shops. Marcy has gone all out. The Manstyle banquet ought to knock her career right over the top. She has imported fifty prewar amber-colored plastic picnic hampers from Oklahoma. At the moment, the chef is packing each with goodies fit for the most successful eligible tycoons in America. Frankly, he is finding the entire affair "*vraiment degueulasse.*" The French, having conquered America, are reluctant to give it back.

      Marigolds, the American flower that grows in each and every state in the U.S. of A., pop out of bar-b-que grills around the room. Golden perfection. And into this perfection will come the best of the best, as per *Manstyle* magazine. The criteria vary. There is no term as debatable as "the best," my dear ones, and each of the editors has his or her favorites.

Marcy surveys her work and dreams of the final touch. "Now all I need is some hunk to jostle my giblets. I spot him from across the room. My heart stops. Without a moment's hesitation, my knight in shining armor strides boldly to my side. He takes me in his arms. He whisks me away."

As fond as I am of Ernest, "Atta girl," say I. Of course she can't hear me. It isn't time. But I appreciate being remembered.

For once, Lizzie, my Lizzie, disappoints me. "You're asking for the impossible. What I want is a decent, workable human being of a guy who knows how to have a relationship."

Marcy offers one of those engaging little snorts. My Lizzie, perhaps anticipating the tenderness of my love, reconsiders. "Maybe you're right. A knight in shining armor might be more realistic."

Forget realism, my loved ones, think—

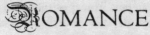

ROMANCE

The limousines arrive just as the picnic baskets are laid before each setting. Marcy and Lizzie await their guests as eagerly as they might await me.

It was Lizzie's idea for both women to dress as sexed-up versions of Dorothy from *The Wizard of Oz*, and Marcy loved it. They are wearing braids and ruby flats and are bustling about. The Harvard Club waiters wear the usual tux, with red bandannas tied at the neck and cowboy hats on their heads. They find it undignified, but they are being well paid for their sacrifice.

When all the guests have taken their seats, Dirk Rapier saunters up to the redbrick camouflaged podium.

"All right. Good evening, you guys." He is shorter and older than Lizzie imagined her childhood screen love to be, and he wears a flesh-colored Band-Aid on his chin. But he *is* Dirk Rapier and he has an aura, a recognizable glow as if he were transparent celluloid and light projected through him.

"I would like to welcome you to the award dinner for award winners. What you have in common is uncommon success, viability, style, and desirability. You are the mega-men of the eighties."

They applaud themselves. In this era of award giving, each of the men present is accustomed to this kind of event. Ever conscious of the television cameras from "Enviable Glitz Tonight," the mega-men smile, their chins lifted or lowered to the most flattering height, no matter what is being said. After the speech, Rapier retires to a back room for a nap.

The Harvard College Crimsonian String Quartet has been engaged to entertain. Marcy considered a country-and-western band, but wanted nothing to take away from her setting. As the "Quartet for Tycoons in E Major" begins, Lizzie catches two specimens of pure hunkismo exchanging mega-glances. Shortly thereafter, they retreat to the elevator shaft. When they return to their seats, Lizzie makes a bet with herself. She deliberately drops a towel and confirms her hunch. These two heartthrobs are holding hands under the table, reducing the eligible tycoon count to forty-eight.

Of the remaining four dozen, one is busy eyeing his reflected image in the glittering cellophane hometown pond, and four are trading the souvenir baseball cards Marcy set at each place setting, leaving a balance of forty-three potential nuggets in what ought to be a gold mine for the only two women in the place.

Marcy has been approached by the food editor of *Manstyle*, who suggests that maybe she ought to do a monthly column. That gives her great pleasure, but it is difficult not to think about those nuggets. If one of those tycoons took a fancy to her, she wouldn't give the old Ern a second thought. It wouldn't particularly matter which one. Each of these men has one quality that Ernest cannot possess: None of them is Ernest.

Lizzie wanders into the kitchen to put her feet up. The French chef gives her a hamburger, and she relaxes. Twelve hours into the day, she is more concerned about her soles than her heart. The last time Lizzie saw a tux was at the junior prom. Each of these men has managed to look unique in black on black with a white shirt: velvet, satin, silk, patent leathers, alligator. Such luxury. Such having. All these haves. "And I am a have-not," Lizzie says out loud.

The French chef brings her a handful of walnuts. "We have. And pistachio, *aussi*. You want anything, I bring." Suddenly Lizzie begins to cry. The chef pats her shoulder helplessly. "You don't like? I take them away."

The evening's work is easing off as the tycoons drift into clusters. Inspired by the decor Marcy worked so hard to design, many of these social zircons are engaged in a rousing chorus of "Ninety-nine bottles of beer on the wall." At "fifteen bottles of beer on the wall," during the Hostess Twinkies course, Marcy finally feels she has been noticed. This is important. Marcy was beginning to feel like the help. Worse, she was beginning to feel invisible.

There is a man in the corner around whom six other men are gathered. Marcy is quite certain that the man in the middle has his eye on her. This group of great men seem to be engaged in some serious conversation. What they are really doing is admiring the snapshots of starlets the man in the center has recently seduced.

"This honey," says the man in the middle, "is Miss Innovative Automotive Parts of Indianapolis. Her motor

45

purrs like a kitten. She gave me a transmission problem. Took me months to get rid of it."

"That's Max Shotz, the movie producer. I'd give six inches off the bottom of my hair to have him look at me the way he's looking at you," comments Lizzie as she places brandy inside the hollowed golden torches of the chocolate Lady Libertys. "Kablam. Instant star of stage and screen."

"Kablam? Why would he be looking at me?" Marcy asks innocently. Lizzie may be a nice girl, but she is only a temporary assistant, and Marcy has certain standards of propriety. Sometimes.

"Go talk to him," whispers Lizzie. "He's a good contact."

To hell with that, thinks Marcy. She admires his Jack Nicholson—style bald spot, his black leather pants under his satin smoking jacket. The guy must be forty-three. He's already a success, so he'll have time to have fun with a nice young thirty-one-year-old. He probably thinks a thirty-one-year-old is nice and young. Or at least nice. Ernie didn't dress like this when he was twenty-three.

"What should I say?"

No time to think. Max Shotz begins a slow, sexy, slightly drunken saunter toward guess who. He picks up a chocolate fly and places it on the tip of his tongue. He draws it slowly into his mouth and licks his lips. Marcy and Lizzie are transfixed by this reptilian performance.

"Hey, which one of you is the good witch and which one of you is the *nice* witch?"

Snatching Defeat
from the
Jaws of Victory

Ern doesn't take kindly to being jettisoned. He'd rather it hadn't happened, and he's pretending it hasn't —quite. He'd like another chance and he has a plan. He will hire a cab, surprise an exhausted Marcy after the Manstyle banquet with roses and a ride to his place, a ride she'll never forget. Damn the torpedoes on this one. It'll be love in the backseat if that's what his lady wants.

Ern squeezes his tight little lawyer's tush into his jeans, and slides into his elegant Missoni knit. He's a hunk if he says so himself.

Meanwhile...

Marcy may be exhausted, but she has plans to recharge her cells. She can't decide which will be better— anticipating her first limo ride, having her first limo ride, or sharing the limo with a hotshot like Shotz. She wouldn't have had the nerve to do it alone—she is, underneath her sleek urban exterior, a sheltered girl from the safe haven of Dix Hills, Long Island, who talks hot but balks a lot—so she persuades her assistant, Lizzie, to go with her. Lizzie would rather go home and go to sleep, but on the off chance Shotz will discover her, she agrees to accompany her temporary boss.

And Shotz, how do you think he feels as he signals to his driver? He is leaving with the only foxes in the joint, four tits to call his very own. He is a self-saturated mini-mogul who knows with the assurance of a true believer that every woman has her price, and he's talking bargains. He figures he ought to be able to get a little three-way hibernation out of the evening. He is a full-fledged member of the slimeoisie who has seen too many movies and hasn't a princely hair on his head.

And what do you think happens next?

Marcy gets into the darkened backseat of the stretch, and Max slithers in beside her. Lizzie has a second thought, but Marcy hasn't yet signed her Busy Bee Time Sheet, and so she makes it a threesome. It's all here: a television, an unlisted cellular telephone, a fully stocked bar, a quadraphonic sound system, and a framed photograph of a dusty gray schnauzer. It's the schnauzer that gets to Lizzie.

Max Shotz covers Marcy's shoulders with his tuxedo jacket.

"How thoughtful," she murmurs.

Lizzie wonders how she is going to get Marcy to sign her time sheet without embarrassing herself beyond all belief. Marcy glances back at the scene of her triumph. Just then, Ernest's taxi speeds to the curb. Ernest jumps out. The Harvard Club is darkened except in the kitchen. The tycoons have gone home to gloat. Marcy slides down in her seat.

Ernest doesn't see her. "Marcy! Marce?" He bangs on

the heavy wooden doors. He figures she's probably in the kitchen.

Shotz looks at him, looks at her, and Marcy opens the door of the limo without waiting for the driver to come around. "Shit. I give utterly up. It's Ernest."

Lizzie has no choice. She reaches across Max's lap to grab Marcy's arm. "I need you to sign this."

Marcy signs. "You were terrif. Thanks."

"If you ever need me..."

"Gotta run," says Marcy, kissing Max's cheek. "Oh, jeez. It was a real pleasure. Sorry I gotta run."

"A big kiss," says Max. He's not wasting his lips on the fox that ran away. He turns his attention to Lizzie, giving her the look that launched a thousand anxiety attacks. She makes a move to get out of the limo, but the driver makes his move first. Max and Lizzie are on the road.

"What are you doing here?" spouts Marcy as she gets into the waiting taxi.

"I thought you'd be tired."

"Oh, Ern, you make General Custer's timing look admirable. That was Max Shotz, the movie producer, and he was going to give me a ride home in his limousine."

Ernest ignores this and places his arms around his estranged intended. "Come on, Marce. Let's talk. Why give up on us when I'm just on the verge of what we've been waiting for?"

"I'm not interested in talking, Ernest. I'm finished waiting, Ernest. I'm not meant for you, Ernest. I'm meant for excitement, movement, speed, mystery. Okay?"

"So you want to go kayaking in the dark?" he offers, ever practical.

"I thought I made this clear. I am exhaustedezvous, and we are kaputsky. Or don't you understand plain English?"

Having lost the battle, Ernest permits himself a bit of

fun. "No last one-night stand, Sitting Bull? I'm more than a little big horny."

Marcy is almost forced to smile, so she uses her emotional memory to think of something rotten—it works.

Lizzie is also thinking of something rotten—Max Shotz. Max Shotz is edging Lizzie farther into the leather recesses of the backseat. He is so close that his five o'clock shadow is making her itch, and the smell of his cologne is inducing nausea. Lizzie desperately rolls the window down and draws the fresh late-night air into her nostrils.

"Come on, Max. Let's talk. Get to know each other. Tell me about yourself."

Max is irritated, but prepared. He presses a button on the remote-control unit. An image gathers on the television screen, and then, as the synthesized violins rise to meet the synthesized French horns and the score begins to take flight, a title fades up: "Max Shotz—The Man."

"Wow," Lizzie murmurs. She can't help it.

Max relaxes. The fox is impressed. He's on his way. "Let's watch. I like to watch." And so they do, as Max's fingers drift purposefully toward Lizzie's cleavage. "Mmm," says Max, with a sidelong inspection of the goods. "I can see you have a lot of talent. You must be an actress."

You know actresses, especially out-of-work actresses; hit them in their vanity and they're putty. Silly Putty. "You can really tell?" wonders the success-starved Lizzie.

Max is doing better than he thought. He moves in for the legendary earlobe-nibble-to-tongue-between-the-breasts play. "Every woman is an actress," he whispers.

Foul. Lizzie doesn't want to hear about every woman. As the limousine stops for a red light, she throws open the door and runs for it. Max jumps out after her. This she did not anticipate. She buries herself deep in a crowd of people. When she reaches the center, she finds herself face to face with a mime.

Bear this mime in mind. He is a mensch. I know him personally, and will someday introduce you. His name is Michael. But Lizzie doesn't know this, and neither does Max, who is doubly excited by his elusive fox, and has plowed through the onlookers to find her.

"Baby—" he begins. Max doesn't know Lizzie's name, and in the darkness, has hardly seen her face.

Michael the Mime spots a subject. He wordlessly mimics Max Shotz, the eligible tycoon movie producer, attempting to discreetly lure his quarry into the waiting trap.

"Baby—"

The crowd laughs and applauds, and for a moment, Max's attention breaks. "Don't you know who I am, you white-faced whippet?" Max takes a swing at the jaw of the agile mime. The laughter and applause of the audience— and their monetary appreciation—will keep Michael the Mime soaring for a week.

Lizzie makes her escape, leaving a bristling, though not entirely humiliated—applause *is* applause—Max to retreat to his limo.

He instructs his driver to stop at the next newsstand and pick up a copy of *Penthouse*. In truth, he prefers his women on the page or on the screen, where they can turn him on and he can turn them off.

The Imagination and
the Kink

Michael's white-faced whippetry has been re-fined over years of practice, and when he works, during the warm seasons, he works day and night. Michael makes no excuses. He does what he does proudly, if at times a bit defensively. Michael the Mime may not be what most people these days think of as a success, but I admire him. He has an unusual courage.

In a city that holds money, position, appearance sacred in equal measures, Michael's job is to be the clown on the steps of the temple. And Michael is somewhat of a nonbeliever when it comes to the aforementioned. He likes comfort, he loves beauty, but security, to him, is an illusion second only to God. Free from the belief that what he owns will protect him from sorrow or harm, he does not own for owning's sake. And he works only at what he loves, on the philosophy that life is short, since we live in the nuclear age. Floating free can be a bit lonely, though. Those about him who are bound and tethered may, if they are a certain sort, admire him, or, if they are not that sort, resent him. Regardless of which way they go, they do not always understand that although Michael does not have *their* values and commitments, he does *have* values and commitments.

Beyond the V- and C- factors, and underneath the white paint, he is also handsome. He has bright green eyes, and the facial structure of a Jewish Indian—high, broad cheekbones; prominent, aristocratic nose. His great grandfather was a merchant who traveled from Minsk to New York and New York to St. Louis. His great grandmother was an Indian girl of considerable beauty and marriageable age. At first, the question of faith concerned Michael's great grandfather, but the Indian girl was sturdy and dark like the girls he had admired in his homeland. Being fair-colored himself, he was drawn to his opposite.

Michael is the same way, which is why he has noticed Susan. After his noon performance in front of the Plaza Hotel, Michael wiped his face into anonymity and wandered over to the Alice in Wonderland sculpture in Central Park to watch the mothers and children, and the nannies and children. Sometimes Michael comes here to imagine another life in which he is maybe not so free, and he is the father who provides for a cluster of carefree, peach-faced children in beautiful doll clothes. And which one of these women would be his wife? He doesn't count the nannies, only the mothers, because as loving as the nannies seem to be, the mothers and the children are physically part of one another. It is odd then, that he decides the woman whom we know to be Susan would be his imaginary wife.

Susan is alone, and she, too, has come to watch families. At the moment, she is in no frame of mind to notice Michael at all, much less to notice his admiration. Something has happened at the office.

Ernest and Susan would rather not have kept the helium-headed cosmetic queen who served as their temporary secretary, but it seemed too much trouble to replace her. Any serious typing could be done down in the goldfish bowl. Susan secretly wondered what the temp could possibly *do* in any other sphere of life, anyway, because of the extraordinary length of her talons. It was, as she figured it, almost an act of charity to employ a woman with three-inch fingernails. What else could she possibly do?

Well, she had apparently done something pretty spectacular. Honoroff, leaping over the personnel department's paperwork—which had kept Ernest and Susan from hiring a full-time legitimate secretary these many months—had just snatched the be-taloned temp and promoted her to his permanent full-time personal assistant. There was no sex involved, or at least no contact.

The story was this: Honoroff was an honorable man on a technicality. A brilliant lawyer, he carried within him a moral esthetic which was highly conscious of laws and obeyance. He did not break the rules, but as a lawyer, he also knew how to bend them. Honoroff did not commit adultery. What he did do, secretly, was conduct a correspondence with Miss Talon through the electronic mail system that connected the computer terminals at W, P & H.

Wednesday, when Miss Talon had been out at lunch, Susan innocently checked the secretary's computer diskette in order to find a document she wished to revise. The documents were cryptically labeled so she did a little guesswork. As she was using the terminal, a light flashed in the corner, indicating that electronic mail was being sent from Honoroff's office, so naturally, she positioned the computer to receive it. At this point Miss Talon returned, and together she and Susan watched Honoroff's explicitly pornographic message fill the computer screen:

AS SOON AS THE JUDGE GOT THE DEFENDANT INTO HIS PRIVATE CHAMBERS, HE GRABBED HER SCANTILY CLAD BODY. "LET ME LICK THAT SWEET LOVE JUICE," HE MURMURED AS HE SLAMMED THE CHAMBER DOOR AND TORE OFF HIS ROBES. THE DEFENDANT RIPPED OFF HER SCANTY CLOTHES, EXPOSING THE MOUTH OF HER SMOOTH-SHAVEN PUSSY. THEIR TONGUES TANGLED IN PASSION AS THE JUDGE MADE A MOTION, SLAMMING HIS HARD MEAT INTO THE WAITING WETNESS...

Miss Talon giggled. "Oh," she sighed to Susan, who was suddenly raw and reeling, "that's much better than the last one!"

Susan felt the veins in her neck begin to pulse. "I presume he is not referring to your cat." Visions of sexual harassment charges pressed against the boss who was championing her hard-won step up to partnership danced in her head. "What are you going to do about this?" Susan choked. At forty-six, Honoroff is so well groomed that his socks are woven to match his suits. Nonetheless, Susan will never again be able to look at her boss without thinking of him as a member of the greasy raincoat brigade.

"Just don't tell him you know. He's so conservative," Miss Talon the temp advised. Then she entered her own electronic mail account and tapped out a response that caused Susan's cotton-clad unshaven you-know-what to wither.

The next day, Miss Talon was made permanent staff, leaving Susan mulling over her sundry quandaries as she meandered in Central Park, unmindful of the gentle fantasies of Michael the Mime.

Susan is trying to think about Life, but she doesn't know what to think. This is an unusual condition. Susan comes well armed with analyses and philosophies for most occasions, but this time she's stumped. She stares at the children and concocts a false memory of the simplicity of childhood. That's all right. It's a romantic idea, and Susan needs to be soothed. Would motherhood be simple? Natural bonds are simpler than professional concoctions. Or is it that they are impossibly more complex and that's why she stayed away from them back in the days when there seemed to be choices to make? She doesn't know what to think. She opens her briefcase and takes out a sandwich she made for herself this morning.

Michael sees the imaginary mother of his children look up from her reverie. He smiles at her, and when she smiles back, he impulsively decides to approach her.

Jiminy Cricket, thinks Susan as she sees a handsome stranger in black clothing coming her way, I hope I'm not about to be attacked by a pervert. She won't take any chances. She smiles once more, timidly, and tries to look relaxed as she scurries back toward the none-too-safe office.

The Honoroff Effect

Inasmuch as I cannot change what is fated, Susan must wait until exactly the right time to meet her true love. I am speaking of myself, and not Michael the Mime, although Michael the Mime is a fine fellow and a bit of a P.C. himself, in many respects. Based on lifelong evidence, his estimation of his own sex appeal is quite high, and he is a bit titillated by Susan's brush-off.

He thinks about her off and on during the rest of the day.

Susan is thinking about how she can continue to respect the venerable Farkas D. Honoroff after reading his amateur effort at pornography. She cannot. It wasn't even skillfully written. She will take Miss Talon's advice and wear her professional blinders. Confessed knowledge of what helped Miss Talon's career would certainly hurt Susan's. Susan would like to confide in someone. She considers telling Ernest, but decides that that, too, would be unprofessional.

When Susan returns to the office, Ernest bores her

with an unprofessionally sorrowful account of the demise of his relationship with Marcy. "And then she said I was too nice and she didn't want anything more to do with me! Can you ferret an iota of logic out of that?"

Susan doesn't answer.

"What's so funny?" Ernest demands. Susan wasn't aware that she looked amused.

"Not a blessed thing, really, Ernest."

"C'mon."

"Well," Susan admits, "I was thinking of a little rhyme. 'She offered her honor, he honored her offer, and all night long he was on her and off her.' Honoroff. Get it?"

"What's the matter with you?" Ernest finds Susan's inattention in his moment of need a bit insensitive. Who will soothe him?

"We need a new temp," says Susan. "You want to call Busy Bee, or should I?"

"I'm too upset. You know, Susan, underneath all this legal prowess beats the heart of a man."

Susan is hysterical enough to have a passing desire to see the chest the heart beats in. "I know. Believe it or not, I have feelings too."

Ernest does not want to hear or believe anything about Susan's feelings. Susan senses this and is wildly embarrassed. She decides to divert attention from herself with another unprofessional sally. "Wanna hear a kinky story?" she begins.

After Ernest recovers the ability to breathe normally, he picks up the phone. As he dials Busy Bee, he notices that Susan's cheeks are a particularly appealing pale fuchsia.

The Plot Thickens

Now, for nine points, who do you think was called to be the new temporary secretary at Witkin, Pritkin & Harris?

After the Max Shotz debacle, Lizzie decided the penalties of promoting her career were either too sharp or too sticky. That morning, she noted that although she had used the Elancyl anticellulite ivy extract cream and rubber massaging mitt for ten days, and she was as smooth as a grape on the surface, lo, when she gathered a handful of thigh, she was as lumpy as gooseberry jam. She knew no statistics on the relation of cellulite to success, but she did know that her starlet-in-high-cut-bathing-suit days were drawing to a close. And, more than that, she was starting not to care. Truth be known, Lizzie was tired of being obsessed with her physical contours. Where did they get her?

She was toying with a new image of herself when the job came in from Busy Bee. Making buckets of dough in a law office fit the short-run scheme. So I admit I am a failure, she thought, I admit that and then I work for six months, save as much as I can, and go to Greece where I have never been. I become an eccentric English teacher who wears a long braid and rides a bicycle and allows her face to weather in the sharp sunlight of the countryside.

Lizzie figures she would live with some Anthony Quinn look-alike who spent long hours in a coffeehouse and long hours in her bed and who treasured her for her foreignness and her luxuriant red hair. He would love her deeply, in part because she was a free spirit who would not marry him.

Lizzie has two business suits she deems appropriate for a law office. If she mixes and matches, she can make it through five respectably dressed days a week, at $13 an hour, for six months, and get away with a gross of more than $12,000. The leftovers after taxes and expenses ought to, if she lives frugally, finance her escape.

When she gets to the office building, she recognizes it as the one her catering boss, Marcy, pointed out to her before the Manstyle banquet. The one where that nice guy who she couldn't stand was a lawyer. Ernest or Arnold, something like that.

By 8:00 A.M. Ernest is usually huddled behind his *Times,* clutching a mug of rose hips tea. This morning, Ernest is under his sheets, immobilized by the realization that Marcy seems to be quite fixed on the disastrous conclusion that their romance is kaputsky. Having spent the entire night replaying highlights of the past year in his head, he has concluded that maybe he ought to have been more demonstrative, and maybe she is an impossible; vile creature for kaputskying him just when he was finally ready to come through. The sex part bothers him. He's no limp dick; he was just preoccupied. He felt more like a man the more successful he was, so he knocked himself out to be the most man he could be, and in the process, he l.d.'d to a certain extent. Jane Pauley would have understood that.

Jane Pauley. Ernest peels the sheets back and raises his head. He spots the television remote control box. He switches on the "Today Show." Ahhhh. Immediately he feels the radiance of Jane's calming presence. Jane— always well groomed, smart but not curt, glowing and collected, even after the babies. And such a straightforward mid-American prettiness. The kind of wife a man could take to the boss's house for dinner. Mr. Honoroff, I'd like you to meet my lovely and talented wife, Jane. But Jane Pauley is already married. Her husband is some lefty comic-strip writer who gives every appearance of being very much alive. It is hard to feel threatened by a comic-strip writer, and as long as said husband remains unseen, he doesn't seem to be much in the way of Ernest's fantasies. If pressed, Ernest would hasten to concede that this husband probably added to Jane's glow and her alluring, heartwarming unattainability. Marcy had never measured up to Jane, Ernest admits to himself in the cold morning light. Jane was network; Marcy would never be more than local. But how could the unworthy Marcy have had the nerve to leave him? He banishes thoughts of Marcy as he watches Jane interview John Updike about his latest upper-middle-class adultery novel. Spunky Jane confesses to a preference for his book reviews. Inspired, Ernest finds the will to get out of bed, get dressed, and get to work.

Susan is earlier than usual on account of the new temp. She wants to be sure that everything gets off onto sure footing, with no stray fashion magazines or pornographic diskettes in the desk. Susan has decided to insist on professionalism, and plans to take the new temp out to lunch ASAP to discuss office do's and don't's. She cannot afford another ticking sex bomb distracting Honoroff's attentions from Ernest's and her promotions to partnership. Oh ho ho no.

Susan appraises Lizzie as she enters the office. Acceptable. Doesn't look at home in a suit, but at least she wears one. Susan formally extends her hand.

"How do you do? I'm Susan Whitbread. You will be working for me and my partner, Ernest Barnes."

"Ernest?" Lizzie thinks this is an even more impossible coincidence than you do. She recoups. "How do *you* do? My name is Lizzie Edmunds."

Acceptable name, thinks Susan.

Lizzie takes the lid off her take-out coffee. "My chief vice. I can't live without coffee in the morning."

"Neither can I," says Susan. Lizzie is quite acceptable.

Ernest lumbers past the both of them and into his office. He shuts the door behind him. Susan performs the introduction. "That was Ernest. He's not usually like that."

A moment later, Ernest reopens the office door. "Excuse me. I was a bit preoccupied."

Ernest nods at the new secretary without particularly seeing her. He is still somewhere between Jane and Marcy, with nary a brain cell to devote to new feminine territory.

I wish I could say that Lizzie was equally oblivious. She is a sucker for a man in a Brooks Brothers suit. Ernest looks remarkably handsome for someone in the depths of a post-breakup depression. Perhaps it is that tired, deprived, haunted, rejected look in combination with the reviews Lizzie had heard while trailing after that blonde caterer. Everything Marcy complained about sounded ideal to Lizzie, who didn't know Marcy well enough to tell her, "Baby, it's even colder outside." Having done some minor calculations on the qualities embodied in this not unattractive stable-hearted lawyer, Lizzie, I am afraid, is quite smitten at first sight. This concerns me. What does she know about this Ernest, really?

You may suspect that I have just experienced a twinge of jealousy. I do not deny it. Prince Charming is never impossibly jealous, never ever. But now and then, I sense I am in danger of seeing you spirited away. And I do rather care for Lizzie, though not nearly as profoundly as I care for you and those beautiful eyes of yours. I am drunk with desire thinking of it. Don't tempt me this way or I will not be able to go on.

Susan and Lizzie
Have a Chat

You know how these things happen. Susan's intention, in sporting for two heavily heaped roast beef sandwiches, was to have a preventative little chat with the new temp about The Way Things Ought to Be Done. By the time she got around to it, she began to have second thoughts about the need for such a chat. Lizzie seemed to be efficient, quiet, and polite. She took off Lord-knows-where most lunch hours, but she was back in time.

As a policy, Susan did not believe it was appropriate for superiors to lunch with subordinates unless there was clearly a mentor relationship or other business-related purpose. Bluntly, she didn't think it did her career as a woman and a lawyer much good to be chummy with secretaries who were, because of the way things are and have been, almost always also women. She wished she didn't feel she needed to feel this way, but she had struggled so hard for recognition, she was not inclined to risk being taken for a member of the typing pool. At W, P & H, even the secs dressed to meld, so Susan carried a briefcase any fellow lawyer could identify as being worth two weeks of secretarial salary. She had an inkling that were circumstances otherwise she might have liked to get to know this Lizzie, and so she went ahead with the lunch, on a business basis, although The Chat seemed beside the point.

Lizzie's thinking on the matter is considerably less complicated. A free lunch with a nice boss. Why not? Being an actress, Lizzie has a flair for knowing how to behave with certain types of people. She had discerned from day one that she ought not reveal her escape plans and thespian aspirations to her employers. You tell lawyers only what they need to know. Besides, her crush on Ernest Barnes has swelled in proportion to his preoccupation with other things. The more his mind is elsewhere, the more she thinks about him. She has become almost unnaturally quiet, polite, and efficient because between her discretion and her emotions, she is thoroughly dammed up and has nothing to say. Lizzie is usually, by her own accounts, as engaged by herself as the next actress. Lunching with Susan, she finds herself playing the role of the exceptionally good listener.

Susan is left to do most of the talking, and soon she surprises herself. "Let me tell you something," she finds herself confiding, "for a bunch of smart guys, lawyers can be pretty stupid when it comes to women. Either you're female or you're a lawyer. If you're a female lawyer, then you're a lawyer. And I'm a lawyer. And my love life is only slightly more extinct than the brontosaurus."

Lizzie swallows a mouthful hastily so she can respond. "I can't believe that. You're surrounded by tons of glorious manhood. You can't tell me that you don't get your fair share of the hunk contingent. You're in a prime spot, Susan."

"I'm telling you. I'm practically invisible."

Lizzie is about to refute this claim as well, but then she stops to think. Ernest has been rather remarkably oblivious of her reliably striking red mane, not to mention the rest of her. Lizzie figured that from the way that woman Marcy from the Manstyle catering job was talking, Ernest might be slightly bruised from sitting in the ejection seat. But even so...

"Maybe there's something strange about lawyers."

"Thanks a bunch, toots." Susan hardly needs to have her insecurities confirmed by this temp, no matter how acceptable she is.

"Not *you!* The ones with the anesthetized lower brains."

"You think it's just men? Sometimes I can't help thinking I send out vibes," confesses Susan. "Underneath this legal exterior lurks...a legal interior. That sort of thing."

Actually, thinks Lizzie, evaluating her new friend's personal style, that may be the case. Susan seems to be one of those women who modeled her personality after those little Russian matryoshkas, hand-painted rosy-cheeked grandmama-shaped boxes that encased themselves in slightly larger, slightly different little rosy-cheeked grandmama-shaped boxes—deep inside was the core Susan, which was encased in the unrefined emotional Susan, which was encased inside the refined emotional Susan, which was encased inside the sexy Susan, which was encased inside the modified Susan, which was encased inside the professional Susan.

"Well, maybe you do cover up a bit?" offers Lizzie tentatively. "Kind of like in Freud?"

"Kind of like Truth or Consequences, if you ask me." Susan slurps at her egg cream with uncharacteristic abandon.

"We'll just have to make 'em notice," Lizzie promises. Already she is making plans, and not only for Susan.

66

Marcy Finds
Personal Fulfillment
Through Her Work

   With Ernest out of her schedule, Marcy has a
lot more time to devote to Individual Culinary Image
Consulting for private customers. She finds this work
fulfilling because in the process of refining the food
images of her affluent clients, she contributes to their
happiness and social standing, hence their personal
fulfillment, hence they tell their most trusted friends,
and hence Marcy gets more work. But in a way she
is an unsung hero. Many a socialite might tell you
that one's Culinary Image is a reflection of one's most
intimate and carefully developed very special personal
style, and so even if one hires a consultant to help, one
wants to, and rightfully should, take full credit and
reap full reward for the results. For, after all, one is
what one eats and even more so what one serves. Marcy
doesn't get invited to the glittering dinners and lun-
cheons she inspires and guides, nor does she get notice
in the society pages. She is an insider's secret. It is no
wonder, then, that she is summoned to the residence of
Ellis Yuppington. Marcy arrives at the gleaming Luxury

Tower. She enters the lush atrium lobby that divides the inside doors from the outside doors, and waits.

Behind a gray curtain, a short man in a gray uniform operates switches and dials that control the several security video monitors keeping watch over Luxury Tower. A screaming teakettle fogs up the screens, and so he turns away to fix himself a bit of Darjeeling. He resettles behind the monitor bank, pulls out a handkerchief, and dabs at the condensed moisture. There is a woman in the lobby. He takes a sip, swallows, and leans toward the microphone. "*Speak!*" he bellows, as he twiddles a dial to deepen the tone and add reverberations.

Marcy cannot see the source of this great and powerful voice. "I . . . I'm here to see Mr. Ellis Yuppington."

The doors part without apparent human aid. The little uniformed man steps out from behind a gray curtain and speaks to Marcy in a baby boy whisper, "May I ask whom wishes to see him?"

"Marcy Lightner. Caterer. We have an appointment."

The little man nods and disappears behind the curtain. "*You may proceed, Mrs. Lightner!*"

"Miss," she corrects, in the general direction of the curtain.

The little giant's "*Sorry*" rebounds off the foyer walls as the trompe l'oeil brushed stainless steel and rosewood elevator whisks Marcy upward to Ellis Yuppington's duplex in the sky.

Ellis Yuppington finds it possible to row on his souped-up Precor machine while he wields his entrepreneurial wand because he has a voice-activated speaker phone and an enormous capacity to control his breathing. He never ever lets his business associates hear him sweat. He takes great pride in his ever evolving physique. Much like the doctors whose unstated desire is not only to thwart, but to actually eliminate death, Yuppington sees exercise not as a bulwark against aging, but as an antidote. Nonetheless, Yuppington hates actually *doing* exercise. He could well afford to pay someone to do it for him, but he has not yet figured out a way to transfer the benefits. Ah, he thinks philosophically, there you have it —negative amortization on the mortgage of life.

"Yo!" he calls as he hears Marcy's knock at his door. "Let yourself in."

Ellis nods in greeting and then continues the conversation he is having with his agent. The interest in Ellis's best-selling self-help book, *Getting Rich Through Having Lots of Money,* has been dropping off recently. The agent is pushing for a sequel, but Ellis has been toying with the spiritual side of entrepreneurship lately—in fact, just this minute. "How 'bout I do a kind of inspirational thing. Negative Amortization on the Mortgage of Life. What do you think? Getting past the Me Generation and into the Post-Me but staying away from this backlash of liberal-do-gooder crap. Huh?"

The agent thinks the title is unnecessarily downbeat, but he agrees to look for a ghostwriter to help round out the concept. Ellis doesn't write his own books. There's no need to overdo.

Marcy shows herself to the kitchen. She begins opening cabinets and is overcome by dismay. This Ellis Yuppington fellow may have a godlike body, but his taste in food disgusts her. She finds cheap caviar, a rotting Swiss cheese sandwich, and a jar of additive-infused peanut butter.

When Ellis extracts himself from his phone conversation, he hurries into the kitchen to meet his consultant.

"Sorry." He isn't the least bit sorry. He believes in keeping people waiting just enough to clearly, but discreetly, assert his power to do so. "It's a pleasure to meet you, Marcy. You come well recommended. Now here's the problem. I'm a busy man, Marcy, and part of my business

69

is staying on top, knowing the trends. I understand that you're number one in food, and that's important to me."

"Thank you," says Marcy graciously. She jots down a couple of notes.

Ellis gestures at the opened cabinets. "I see you've done some research. Good work. I used to be able to get by on a knowledge of wine. But alcohol is outish. I knew my way around the restaurants. Now, my assistant has recently pointed out to me that there are certain culinary accoutrements that the young urban professional is expected to have at home." Ellis leaves the room for a moment and returns with a file folder. Consulting the folder, he continues, "For instance, rosemary vinegar. Herbs de Provence . . ."

"Last season completely, I'm afraid. If you've read about it, it's probably already out," Marcy observes.

"Well, you know better than I. At any rate, my assistant, Magenta, was just clipping relevant articles and so forth for referral. You're the professional. Marcy, I want this kitchen to have the right stuff."

"Piece of cake," she assures him. She means, of course, not the usual layer cake but triple crème fraîche and chocolate mousse with wild strawberry torte. Flipping to a new page in her notebook, she holds her pen in the ready position. "Now. I'd like to ask you a few questions about your preferences."

"The hot condiments, that's all."

"So. You like spicy food? Indian is enjoying a resurgence."

"I mean hot as in hip, Marcy. Upscale, up-to-date, the best. Indian is fine."

"But is there anything you especially like?"

Ellis grows serious. "There are more important things at stake than my personal taste, Marcy. I want the kitchen that reflects the life-style a sensitive man of my stature and refinement is supposed to have."

With that, Ellis opens the jar of peanut butter and takes a finger full. Marcy stifles a sigh. How can she expect to be elevated and utterly fulfilled by her work when she is faced with the uninhibited consumption of polytetrahydrologized peanut butter?

W, P & H: Everyone
Is in a Good Mood
at the Same Time

Weight loss and the discovery of untapped resources of nervous energy are frequent side effects of romantic distress, which is why, my darlings, those whose time has come to reap the joys of love with their Prince Charming have a pleasing roundness about them—and an assured serenity. They have contentment and passion together. They can relax.

Because he is a man, Ernest is not in my jurisdiction, but I observe him closely. I note that romantic distress has spurred him to make, or at least will, certain changes in himself. For one, he has decided to be bolder. To this end, as he leaves his apartment for work, he puts on his new weathered leather jacket over his suit. He swaggers to the subway stop feeling magnetic. He dares to slip a pair of red-framed, super-chic sports-star sunglasses over his eyes.

Standing underground in the darkened subway station, he finds that it is nearly impossible to see. He sacrifices the Jim McMahon look and puts the glasses back in his pocket. But that's the kind of disappointment Ernest can take in his stride.

Lizzie is feeling cozy. Yesterday Ernest greeted her by name for the first time. It happened that it was the wrong name; he had called her Jane. But it was progress. It meant he knew she existed in a female form. The rest she could work on. Toward the end of being noticed more accurately, she stopped at the Dumas bakery for a dozen caramel pecan breakfast rolls. We're talking sublime caramel pecan breakfast rolls.

She's in the office a few minutes early, but already she hears murmurs from behind Susan's closed door. Sounds like Honoroff's in there.

Lizzie arranges her pecan rolls and settles in to eavesdrop.

"...And after a review of his last deposition, the likelihood of a successful plea against our client out of court seems next to nil," Susan says forcefully.

"Good point, Susan. And one we might have overlooked," Honoroff responds. "You're a team player. In fact, I might say you're one of our best men."

Lizzie can't hear Susan's response.

Ernest makes an entrance. Lizzie thinks he must have damaged his overcoat, because he is wearing some ratty leather number over his suit.

"Morning..."

"Lizzie," she says helpfully, holding out a plateful of premeditated temptation. Ernest helps himself.

"You bake these?"

"Unfortunately, no."

Ernest takes a bite. He has never been as orally gratified as he is at this moment. He takes a good look at his benefactress. "You cook?"

"No. But I order a mean pizza."

73

"Good," Ernest decides. "I can't stand women who cook. Jane Pauley doesn't cook. Nope, not her. That's good. I don't trust a woman who cooks."

"Well I promise you..."

Ernest pulls his red-framed shades out of his pocket and places them over his eyes as he pirouettes so that Lizzie can fully appraise his leather jacket from all sides. "What do you think?"

"Very nice," Lizzie says in an insincerely ladylike tone.

Ernest wants more. "Does it make a difference? Spruce up the old image?"

"Actually," Lizzie ventures, "I think you're fine the way you are."

Ernest is taken aback. It has been at least nine years since he's heard anyone besides his mother utter that phrase. During his own shocked silence, he hears the muffled sound of the voices behind closed doors. "What's up?"

"Honoroff."

Ernest whips off his glasses and his jacket and thrusts them into the coat closet. "Holy herd of Holstein cows, why didn't you say something? He coulda seen me like that!"

Lizzie shrugs. She could ask him why he was dressed up like some Brat Packer in the first place, but she doesn't think that would be a tactful question. Ernest knocks on Susan's door.

Honoroff has been almost unnaturally chipper since Ernest and Susan's former temp, that titsy cosmetic queen with the talons, was moved to his office. He feels young, energetic, and yet—as the marital equivalent of a technical virgin—pure. In some small way he credits Ernest and Susan with his new happiness. Perhaps that is why he has finally moved ahead with their promotions.

As Susan looks on, Honoroff claps his hand across

Ernest's back. "Well, here you are. I've got a little something I've been waiting to say. Congratulations to the both of you—partners."

It is that simple. Ernest and Susan are gracious and calm and as happy as two cats with six lamb chop bones. Honoroff knows that that's how they're feeling. He was there once, himself. "If you'll accept a little advice—"

"Yes, sir?" the partners chime, becoming immediately self-conscious about their words spewing out in unison. Ernest clears his throat to differentiate himself. Susan takes a seat.

"Take the rest of the day off. A certain percentage of relaxation is important."

And so they will. And so will Lizzie—with pay. But first the three of them delve into the pleasures of sugar shock as delivered to them by four pecan rolls apiece.

The Effects of Unanticipated Free Time

Lizzie has been an unemployed actress long enough not to let a few hours of unforeseen liberty rattle her. Between them, Ernest and Susan have probably had five days of unscheduled time—total—in the past decade, so Honoroff's dictum presents a challenge. Neither one wants to admit to being incapable of pleasurably frittering away an afternoon, so each tells the other that they have errands to run.

As they step onto the street, Ernest and Susan break in different directions, and stride purposefully to opposite street corners. Safely out of view, Ernest stops. His natural urge is to phone Marcy and tell her the news he had been waiting to tell her for the past year. Suspecting that the urge is misbegotten, he vigorously fights it until he spots a telephone booth beckoning him like a siren. He is merely a man of flesh and bones. He succumbs.

Susan has a vague idea that she ought to treat herself. She has made Partner. That's what she wanted. She thinks that she should feel very, very good. She feels sort of good, and hopes that the rest will hit and she will be overcome with joy or something. But what she feels most at the moment is uneasiness. She doesn't really want to be alone, but she doesn't have anyone to be with right here and now in midday Midtown. Susan can't hold a thought in her head. The palms of her hands are cold. Her legs, however, seem to be in fine fettle, so she follows them, and finds herself on the ground floor of Bloomingdale's, where she is pulled toward the warmth of the crowds who gather around the cosmetic counters. Smells and colors. Names. Obsession. Poison. Seductress. Tigress. Euphrates. There is one message, and one message only. Susan hears it. Now that she has risen to the pinnacle of her career, the other challenge emerges like a naked hussy, unshielded by the protective distraction of ambition. Susan is left with Susan. She hears a saleswoman ask her a question, and she nods an anxious yes. The woman leads her to a barstool. Taking Susan's face in her hands, she directs Susan's attention to a mirror.

"There. You see the undertone in your skin is ochre. We counterbalance this by using a Tuscan Apricot base before applying the foundation."

Susan submits quietly to a beauty makeover. Susan turns to the right, to the left, looks up, looks down, as she is told. She cannot get a good look at her perpetual motion Pygmalion until the transformation is complete. Then the woman says, "So."

Susan looks for herself in the mirror. Yes. She's there, though unrecognizable. Susan smiles at the woman and her alien face smiles with her.

"Thank you very much."

The woman lines up nine or ten faux-granite cardboard boxes full of different colored powders and creams and Susan obediently hands over her credit card. Susan wonders how she will duplicate the work that has been done on her, but figures that owning the powders and creams is a start.

I must say that I don't think Susan needs a Tuscan Apricot base. Prince Charming loves her the way she is. While I am not one of those men who needs to view a woman covered in paint in order to find her beautiful, nor am I the sort of man who has no patience for makeup at all. I know that often makeup does make a woman feel the beauty she already possesses within her. Whether or not you wish to ornament yourself with cosmetics, you may rely on me to be fully appreciative. I need not remind you that it is difficult to find exactly the kind of appreciation a woman needs and deserves in the realm of the ordinary man. But then, my darlings, I know that is why you wait for me, and I, I hunger for you. *XX.*

Susan allows herself to feel radiant. She half wishes the temp, Lizzie, were here to evaluate the effect and reassure her. But she has no time to dwell on that. Now that Susan is fully made-up the strolling perfume merchants, who earlier allowed her to pass unnoticed, identify her as a prospect. Susan sees a man who carries an opened umbrella over his head and a satchel over his shoulder. "Aramis," he says as he sprays the air with a spicy cologne. "For the man in your life." Susan hurries away from this imbecile. Doesn't he know that an umbrella opened indoors is bad luck? And what is this business about the man in her life? Busybody.

A beautiful young woman with the curls of Botticelli's Venus stands near the escalator strewing rose petals. She is wearing a wedding gown and murmuring, "Beautiful. Beautiful." Susan approaches. Venus hands her a tiny vial with the word *Beautiful* inscribed on the side. Susan places the vial in her purse as she continues her wandering.

A man in a yellow baseball jacket springs into her path. Squirting the air in front of her face he cries, "Giorgio!"

Susan is startled, but quickly recovers her manners. "Susan."

78

"Giorgio. Giorgio of Beverly Hills!" he exhales.

Susan decides he's a crank and turns away. But she cannot escape. A woman in an identical yellow baseball jacket obstructs her route. "Giorgio!" she cries.

Susan shakes her head no and backs away. This only arouses the Giorgio team, whose zeal is doubled by the challenge of a nonbeliever. Their evangelical mission cannot be thwarted by mere consumer will, because theirs is a cause in which the whole is greater than the sum of the parts. They will not rest until Susan is baptized by the exclusive perfume that everybody's wearing, on or off Rodeo Drive—whether they want it or not. Perhaps she does not fully understand the loneliness of being out of synch with the scent of America. It's for her own good that the Giorgio team heightens its pursuit. "Giorgio! Giorgio! Giorgio! Giorgio! Giorgio! Giorgio! Giorgio! Giorgio! Giorgio!" They spray. She runs. They chase. Susan finds her way back to her Pygmalion and ducks behind the counter until the coast is clear. She reeks of Giorgio, but she is safe. It is then that she catches a reflection of her made-over face in a window of black glass. Like an infant who is newly able to identify the baby it sees in the mirror, Susan is so fascinated she forgets about the Giorgio twins entirely.

She hails a taxi. As she settles into the backseat, the driver opens a window, and a fresh breeze clears the air for them both as she heads home to Blackwatch Towers. Julio's nostrils flare as Susan whizzes past him.

"Susing. You are very different today," he observes.

Susan takes that as a compliment. Susan has learned a new lesson. One way to be noticed is to wear dizzyingly overpowering perfume and a color-highlighted face.

Julio could have told her that. His wife has been doing it for years.

The Consequences of
Ernest's Phone Call
to Marcy

Ernest's spontaneous phone call to Marcy takes some doing. The line is busy. Actually, Marcy has to be talking to two people at once, otherwise Ernest's call would come through the call-waiting system that she had installed so that she'd never miss an opportunity. Her assumption was that she would have a maximum of two opportunities at the same time. Ernest's call presents itself as Marcy's unknown opportunity.

Having braved rejection to make the call in the first place, Ernest is now headily determined not only to dial, but to make complete contact. Filled with what-the-hell, Ernest convinces himself that not only is it a fine idea to convey his happiness to his ex, but that in light of this long awaited triumph, she will want to share his happiness, her body, and her life with him after all. He is willing to take her back without so much as a reprimand.

Only the impulse to change into his Marithe & Francois Girbaud destroyed jeans delays him from hurrying to her side. It is a worthwhile detour. Wearing his destroyed jeans, he appears to be the relaxed fellow he is not. Ernest ignores the nervous pounding of his heart. He reads that as joy, excitement. It is anxiety.

And rightly so.

Marcy is exhausted from a busy week. The Yuppington job has involved hours of rummaging through spice bins, and she is still far from finished. She has argued with Ellis that he must learn how to use the condiments he acquires, and they have compromised on a quick at-home basic course, which Marcy is to conduct in two hours. She doesn't know heaps about Indian cookery herself, but fortunately she is a quick study and, if there are no interruptions, will appear to be on top of things when Ellis walks in the door.

The visit is to be purely professional. Since her breakup with Ernest, there have been virtually no sexual sparks. Ellis doesn't ignite her, nor she him. She catches the eye of the occasional handsome stranger but that is it. She is a little disappointed that romance and excitement have not yet noticed she is ready for them, but not at all discouraged. She has mega-plans. It is more pleasant to mull over the plans that will lead to personal ecstasy than to memorize the recipe to Chicken Mountbatten Wallah with banana date chutney, and she has to force herself to concentrate.

Because she is expecting a delivery man, Marcy has instructed Julio that if a man carrying a package calls to see her, he should send the man along without bothering to ring her on the intercom. When Julio spots Ernest carrying a striking bouquet of forty-eight red roses, he grins.

"*Muy bueno,*" he murmurs admiringly.

Even I am impressed by this gift which is unmistakably in the style of Prince Charming.

Ernest is feeling irresistible and reckless. On this afternoon of his promotion, he's thrown proverbial caution to the proverbial wind, at last—and at the exactly wrong time.

It pains me when a woman I love behaves cruelly toward a besotted suitor, but it so often happens. There seem to be two conditions which provoke this behavior: either (A) she feels she must undertake the dreadful task of ridding herself of the attentions of a man whom she had mistakenly identified as me—*after* she realizes her mistake, or (B) she is faced with Mr. Altogether-Wrong-from-the-Start.

Ernest hurries down the hallway to Marcy's apartment with much the same excitement I felt when at last I had found Sleeping Beauty, or was it Snow White? Anyway, it was some time ago. There are a couple of books out on those two. We'll look it up together, later.

The love Ernest bears as his gift has overflowed the confines of his body. He is ready. Marcy hears what she takes to be the delivery man's knock and sets down her cookbook. She opens the door.

Ernest proffers his roses. "I got it!"

"Got what? What are you doing here? You can't just stop by my apartment like this. What if I was with someone, Ernest?" Marcy scolds. She gives her ex the once-over and decides that he is scrawnier than she remembered.

Ernest has been soaring too close to the sun, and now his feathers are singed and his wings melted to useless stubs. Perhaps, he thinks, I knew this was coming. Perhaps that flutter was not love after all. His eyes water before he can stop them.

"I made partner. I thought you'd want to know."

Marcy softens, but only slightly. She gives Ernest a dry kiss on the cheek, but does not accept his flowers. She does not want to mislead him into thinking there is any hope at all. "That's wonderful, Ern," she says sincerely. "I'm really, really happy for you."

Ernest presses his brain into service, forcing himself to exhibit his teeth in imitation of a smile despite the fact that Marcy has just propelled him past love, pain, and humiliation into a new stratum of emotion—ultra-void numbness. "Well, I just thought you'd like to know."

"I'm really glad you told me, Ernie. That's really great. I'm glad you stopped by," Marcy babbles. "Thanks for stopping by again. And congratulations."

As she shuts the door, Marcy feels herself on the verge of tears. Instead of crying, she dials the butcher shop. "Where the hell is that chicken I ordered!" she demands to know.

Ernest shuffles to the elevator. He can't bring himself to go home alone alone alone on this day that was meant to be one of the great days of his professional life. He's supposed to be celebrating. He can't bear to walk past Julio carrying the flowers that Marcy refused to accept. He can't tolerate the thought of throwing hundreds of dollars worth of sense-swelling, velvety crimson buds into the incinerator.

Ernest decides to find Susan. He goes to the floor he thinks is hers and cannot tell one closed door from another. He takes the elevator to the laundry room. There is a pay phone, as he suspected.

Once again, Ernest dials. This time, without fear.

It is more than likely that Susan would have removed her makeup and her glamorous sweater had she been expecting company, but she is pleased that circumstances are what they are as she opens the door to welcome her new partner.

"Hi," says Ernest weakly. "Could you use some flowers?"

He is so overcome with his defeat that he does not notice her dramatic makeup, nor her scent, nor the alluring softness of Susan's seashell pink angora sweater.

Susan can see that Ernest is distressed, and she assumes that he suffers from more or less the same vague sense of dislocation that she does. She knows that he has come to her for comfort, and she is damned happy to have a bit of companionship, herself. They sit together on Susan's puffy couch watching "Live at Five" and drinking hot cocoa. Neither asks the other how the afternoon was spent.

Later They Go
for a Drink

After "Live at Five" came "News at Six." By 7:30, Ernest and Susan were thoroughly informed and giddily relaxed. Having eaten the few munchable items in Susan's apartment and exhausted the humor of drawling "Howdy, pardner" to each other as they swaggered around the living room, they are separately surprised to find that it isn't yet time to say good-bye.

Without immediate distraction the question arises in Susan's mind as to what will happen next. She finds herself wondering how she looks in the light of the gooseneck halogen lamps she bought to avoid eye strain. She suspects that they do not provide a romantic glow. She considers turning one of the lamps off so that the light is more flattering, but she can't bring herself to do that. It would seem so...suggestive.

Ernie feels the sudden need to stretch his legs. He shakes his arms with exaggerated vigor and draws an unnecessarily deep breath.

"Well. Time for some fresh air, wouldn't you say?"

Susan hurries to agree lest she seem to want to stay

alone with him, here, in her apartment, not lonely alone like before, but cozily alone, just the two of them, as the evening looms languorously before them. And even if she did want him to stay, which she does, she doesn't want to think about wanting him to stay because it makes her unbearably nervous.

The city glimmers like cut crystal, and the night breeze tingles like a swallow of champagne. Ernest and Susan stroll across town and along Fifth Avenue, skirting the dark lushness of Central Park. The Metropolitan Museum of Art towers white and cold as a deserted Greek temple, making the brandy light from the windows of the American Stanhope Hotel irresistible. They head for the elegant bar immediately left of the lobby. Ernest orders Perrier straight up. Susan goes for a scotch and water. Her father taught her to appreciate scotch as a little girl. When she was teething, he rubbed Chivas on her gums, and when she first began to menstruate and suffered awful cramps, he mixed a little Glenfiddich with her milk. When Susan reached eighteen, her father told her the facts of civilized life: It is a sin to dilute your whiskey with water or ice. Susan has taken her father's wisdom as her own until tonight. She asks for water in her whiskey because she doesn't want this Perrier-drinking partner of hers to think she takes her scotch straight. He might draw the wrong conclusions.

As it is, Ernest asks, "How can you stand that stuff? It tastes like medicine to me."

Susan smiles mysteriously. She knows she looks good in the light cast by the candles flickering on the tables and in the sconces above them. They talk about the American Indian paintings on the wall. Since neither knows much about the northeastern tribes, they soon lapse into a comfortable silence.

Susan surveys the tables behind them. She sees a businessman reviewing a prospectus. She sees several stewardesses sitting with stewardess friends, confiding and laughing and sampling pastel-colored drinks that get made in a blender. They seem to be talking about men, and Susan is tempted to eavesdrop, but whenever the speaker gets to the good stuff, she lowers her voice.

Ernie watches gleaming bubbles follow the convection currents in his glass. It helps him to organize his thoughts. "Susan?"

"Yes?" she says tenderly, putting her hand on his coat sleeve.

"Tell me honestly, Susan, man to man, do you think I'm boring?"

Susan ponders the question a polite microsecond. "Nearsighted, but not boring."

Ernest takes a contemplative sip. "What it was, was: She never gave it all to me. For more than two years, she never gave it all to me, so when I lost it, I'd never had it. And that's what hurts."

"Uh-huh." Susan is wounded. She inspects her cleavage. It's still there.

Susan recalculates her plans for the evening and raises a finger. The bartender hurries to her side. "I'll take a triple-rum San Andreas Shake-up, please. Straight up." Susan's revised thinking goes this way: If Ernest insists on nattering on about his ex, she will be better off blunting the effects with a stiff one. If, on the other hand, Ernest realizes that he is seated next to the one woman who might truly understand him, and if he decides to make something of this revelation, she had better have had a stiff one to brace herself for the—please permit me to indulge myself a moment here—stiff one that may follow. There. I said it and it's over.

"Another Perrier, sir?" asks the bartender, as he stifles a sneer.

Ernest shakes his head neither yes nor no. Once again, he is dreamily elsewhere.

"He's had enough," snaps Susan.

Ernest, who is preoccupied, does not feel the sting of Susan's barb, but rises out of private depths to return to the conversation. "There has got to be a woman who appreciates me for all my hidden qualities. But where do you find a good woman in this damned city?"

Susan looks in the direction of the stewardesses for some kind of support in her moment of need. She shrugs. They shrug, and return to their drinks. Susan decides to savor her San Andreas Shake-up for what it's worth. Somewhere in the night bells chime the midnight hour.

"We'd better be going," says Susan, giving Ernest a chance to pick up on her ambiguous "we" and redeem himself.

Outside there is a light drizzle, and the lovers riding past the hotel in horse-drawn carriages snuggle close to each other under blankets provided by the discreet tuxedoed drivers. Ernest hails Susan a cab.

He leans over as Susan slides into the backseat. "I had a great time," he says.

"So did I," says Susan, who continues to slide in order to show Ernest that there is enough room for two.

"Talk to her for me, will you?" he pleads.

"No," Susan responds, disguising her irritation with a sensible tone. "Get over it. Get on with your life. Quit pounding on one closed door when so many others are open to you. It's tedious. It's wasteful. And you're too good for that!"

Ernie takes Susan's declaration at face value. He realizes that he has never fully appreciated Susan's friendship and her well-sculpted character. He realizes that he can rely on her in times of need not only professionally, but personally. She is solid. She is warm. She is honest. She is fun to be with. He does not, however, realize that Susan is a woman. And my darlings, I must tell you frankly, given his lawyerly blind spot, there is a chance that he never will.

Because *her* sorrows are *my* sorrows, this offends me as it offends Susan. I know that on some occasions a woman wants to be wanted by even those men she chooses not to want. And if a woman *does* want a man, well, then ...Susan is not in the mood to view being passed over as an opportunity to wait for me without distraction.

Although I am under strictest orders from Aphrodite *not* to tamper with love before it is time, I cannot resist a slight deviation designed to test, if you will, whether or not the time has indeed arrived to bring love, passion, and good cheer to the dear, if currently slightly soggy, Susan.

As quickly as I think the thought, her taxicab is transformed into a motor-powered pumpkin coach lined with velvet cushions of the deepest forest green. I become the coachman who carries my precious cargo through the dark urban caverns to her home. I can do nothing about the sad fact that Susan, in her current state of mind, does not so much as glimpse her driver, and chooses to interpret the miracle that has presented itself to her as the result of consuming, on a relatively empty stomach, enough alcohol to scrub down a surgical team.

And so you see that at times even Prince Charming joins the linked chain of rejectees. I am not angry with Susan for failing to recognize me. The sad truth is, it happens as often as not. I understand this perfectly. It simply isn't time. I do hope, though, my darlings, that when I come to you, you will not avert your eyes as she has done. But then I know you wouldn't do that. I cannot even entertain the thought.

Ernie Interprets
Susan's Advice

There is an idea lurking just below Ernie's conscious mind. It teases him. It half-suggests itself. But it does not rise to the surface. It persists, like an itch in an unreachable place. The idea will not come and relieve him, nor will the hint of it subside enough to allow him to fall asleep.

Ernest lumbers into the living room and switches on the television. Wrapped in his red plaid robe, he settles onto the cold leather couch. Soon he is staring rapturously ahead, bathed in the glow and flicker of a late-night movie.

Norma Shearer's lips quiver as she swishes across the marble floor of the baronial mansion that was left to her husband by his first wife, now deceased but not forgotten. "Dahling," Norma begins, in the unidentifiably aristocratic accent preferred by screen goddesses of the thirties, "you...ah the one I turn to. Sew strong, sew mahnly, a sheltah from the stohrms of life. Sew wise, and yet...so veddy exciting beneath thet consehvative exteriah...."

The black pencil mustache over Lord Windsorworthy's lip gleams as he and Ernest gaze adoringly at the satin-sheathed Norma, Lady Windsorworthy. She blushes. She hesitates. Lord Windsorworthy offers mahnly encouragement. "Yes, my dyeah?"

"But, but, but—" she stammers, as Lord Windsorworthy and Ernest swell with admiration for this endearingly girlish trait, "But my, my, haht, my passion . . . belongs . . . to . . . anothuh!"

Sundering his identification with Lord Windsorworthy, Ernest ruthlessly stabs the off-button on his remote-control switch. "Suffer, bitch."

At this angry utterance, Ernest feels a rush of freedom. Suddenly things become clear. He need not suffer. The idea rises like Venus on the Half Shell. Susan was right! He should go on! He would pine for Marcy no longer! If he had loved once, he could love again—and well. There was, in this wide world, a worldly woman who would love him, and to whom he could bring his love without fear of betrayal. And if Jane Pauley wasn't free, it would have to be some other fine feminine creature. He was ready, now. He could do it. And yes, he would do it, by jove. Yes, by jove. The movie had left him feeling slightly British.

The next morning, after a rejuvenating sleep, Ernest strides jauntily into W, P & H. In the elevator to the eleventh floor, he accepts congratulations on his promotion with confident grace.

As he enters the office he has occupied with Susan Whitbread since their early days as associates, the office in which they have shared trials and now triumphs, he notices something dramatic and different.

Wait a moment so that the singing angels can warm up for a round of heavenly choruses. The bouncy cherubs will strum their harps as soon as they can get into position. Now:

In the softly diffused morning light, her hair falls delicately on her shoulders in waves of rust and gold, as if she has been anointed by the sun itself. Her skin seems the color of fresh farm cream. Ernest wants to touch her cheek. The turquoise sweater she wears is modest, but manages in a subtle and ladylike way to suggest the sweetness of her breasts. This new temporary secretary, this Lizzie, is quite a lovely little item, indeed. Quite.

She must have changed, concludes the appreciative Ernest, who, in honor of the occasion of falling into admiration so very soon after he resolved to do so, allows himself to feel pleasurable pride in being an especially observant man.

Marcy Plans
to Beat Love
at Its Own Game

Marcy was unsettled by the pang she felt when she turned Ernest and his armload of blossoms away from her door. I am finished with Ernie, but maybe I could have been, should have been—no, maybe he could or should have been—what? Completely different, that's what. If we were two completely different people, things would have worked out between us, she thinks. Having sent Ernest out of her life, she will not tolerate him bouncing back to her, nor will she tolerate the accompanying pangs.

In order to ensure against pangs, because she has had it absolutely up to her tush feathers with pangs, she will have to be in love with at least one main person and one backup person from now on. And she will only be in love if the men in question are exactly right and if it isn't going to be a drag and if it is both thrilling and safe.

She thinks she yearns for Prince Charming, but we know, don't we, my dearest ones, that she has forgotten how the fairy tales go if she's thinking in multiple numbers. If you check the literature you will certainly find that she who has found her Prince Charming has no backup squeezes, and needs none, I proudly add. Living happily ever after is no part-time thing. If Marcy truly wished for me from the bottom of her heart, as we say in the profession, I might at this very moment be sweeping her into my strong, sheltering—but never confining—arms. Unfortunately, the bottom of her heart is dusty with wayward feelings all bunched up together into an uncomfortable clot through which no such wish could travel—yet.

I have climbed too many briar bushes, and scaled too many fortress walls, to give up hope for the likes of Miss Marcy Lightner all that easily. Regardless of my own good faith, Marcy is not presently inclined to bide time waiting for what she considers to be the random appearance of true love, and so she contemplates her plans.

1. She plans to start jogging around the Central Park Reservoir, where she can strike up conversations with men whose muscled bodies she has already been able to appraise. This plan cannot go into action until the weather is a touch warmer. The mornings hold a chill these days and the eligibles are likely to be swaddled in baggy and deceptive sweat clothes.

2. She plans to try to drum up a few consulting jobs in the lux-ier areas of Long Island so that she can ride the Long Island Railroad. She hears that commuter trains are a wonderful place to meet men, but she has to wait until next summer for that because Marcy wants to meet only wealthy and powerful men who are commuting between their Hampton or Montauk beach houses and their glittering New York penthouses. There are some other problems with this plan: The majority of LIRR commuting males, regardless of their other charms, do not meet the above qualifications and the commute that Marcy is considering would involve about six hours round trip, with no guarantee of success.

3. She plans to stop by Love at First Sight, a take-out video dating boutique in Chelsea, so that she can literally screen potential companions before she commits to committing time to getting together with relative unknowns she might like to know. This she can do any season for a high membership fee.

4. She feels that while she has been putzing around with Ernie, developments of which she is not aware may have been made in the world of romance. She wishes to approach the business of taking lovers with state-of-the-art information at her fingertips, and so she plans to take a few of the courses she has seen offered in the Personal Growth Center bulletin.

Marcy decides to take care of items 3 and 4 first. Beyond that, she decides to step up her attendance at wine-tasting events and museums, despite her feeling that it is difficult to find a man whom you have just seen swilling and spitting out mouthfuls of wine sexually attractive, and the only people who tend to bump into her at museums seem to be old women eager for conversation, and pickpockets.

For reasons she does not completely understand, she picks up the phone and dials W, P & H. When the temp, whose voice she does not recognize, answers the phone, Marcy asks for Susan.

"May I tell her who is calling?" asks Lizzie in her official secretarial drone.

"Tell her it's Jane Smith," says Marcy.

When Susan picks up the line, she says, "May I help you?"

Marcy says, "It's me. Marcy. What's up?"

"Nothing much," says Susan who doesn't want to get into it.

"How's everything?"

"Fine, fine."

"How's Ern?"

"Oh, you know. . . ."

"That's good," says Marcy, who doesn't know whether it's good or not or whether she really wants to know how Ern is or why she is asking in the first place. "Hey! What I was really calling about was to see whether you'd like to meet me for lunch sometime next week. I kind of used to like to do that, but now that Ernie and I are, uh—well I can't just drop by the office anymore, and I was thinking. . . . Well, you don't have to tell me, but, you're not seeing anyone seriously these days, are you?"

"Nope. Not that I know of," says Susan.

"Good. I mean, I was looking for someone who was really single to come with me to a couple of things that sound like they might be a lot of fun."

"I don't know," says Susan staring out her window. "I don't really go in for singles things."

"How do you know if you don't try it?" pleads Marcy, who doesn't mind going by herself to Love at First Sight, but would really rather not go to the Personal Growth Center classes without a friend for moral support.

"Why don't we meet for lunch next Wednesday. I'd love to see you anyway," offers Susan.

"Perfect, then," murmurs Marcy. "I can't wait."

Susan has to say what's on her mind. "Uh—" is as far as she gets.

"Oh, don't worry," reassures Marcy, who knows exactly what Susan is getting at. "He's history. We won't mention him at all."

Susan needed the better part of a morning to bury her feelings for Ernie and does not want to disturb the ground in which they lie. "Needless to say," she says.

That Fateful Wednesday:
Part I

As soon as he recognized his attraction to Lizzie, Ernest set about researching the prospects for a relationship in an elaborate and methodical manner, which did not include asking her directly for a date.

There were several matters which needed to be clarified. First, was she otherwise involved? Second, where did she disappear during her lunch hours? Points one and two could have been clarified with a simple question, but a simple question would suggest that Ernest had an interest in Lizzie which exceeded professional friendliness. Third, would she receive a romantic advance from a lawyer in the firm, in particular this lawyer, as an unwarranted invasion of her personal privacy? Fourth, would he, upon making his move, discover that he was wrong to have made it (she might have faults he could not live with, or she might find him a bore), and as a result suffer either disappointment or rejection, either one of which would complicate—as in fact a successful romance would complicate—the work situation. He could not bring himself to fire her simply in order to ask her for a date. The implications! The implications! Poor Ernest suffered for days from a bad case of hypotheticalitis.

But all was not as bleak as I have made it sound. Ernest also dwelt in the heaven of unlimited possibility. He fantasized about the softness of her skin, and how, if she were possessed of such a velvetlike facial complexion, the softness between her thighs must surpass the softness of an angora kitten, and beyond that—what color would it be? Probably strawberry blonde, dreamt Ernie—beyond that softness... Once or twice, as the unsuspecting Lizzie sat only a few feet away, Ernest found himself lodged behind his desk with an awkward erection.

It seemed to me that Lizzie would never have the chance to succumb to her ersatz Prince Charming, because he would never risk removing his romance with Lizzie from the theoretical state that tortured him and placing it in motion.

This was fine with me. But something happened which I did not anticipate.

On Monday, Lizzie, who maintained a crush on the above character, made an offhand remark about having no social life. Ernest snatched the opportunity to say, "Surely, a woman like you must have lots of boyfriends!"

To which Lizzie significantly replied, "Oh, I date now and then. But not often anymore. It seems like a waste of time because none of them is the right one."

"What would be right, if you don't mind my asking?"

"Someone stable. Secure. Someone who knew what he wanted and how to get it. Someone...oh, I don't know."

Ernest transcended his reservations to ask if she took an exercise class during lunch hours and nearly botched the maneuver.

"Why? Do you think I need one?" retorted the almost offended Lizzie.

"Oh, no. I just noticed you seemed to have some-where to go at lunchtime."

"Oh, yeah, I do sometimes," answered Lizzie. Although her answer didn't satisfy Ernest's curiosity, he was pleased with most of Lizzie's testimony. Lizzie had vowed to herself that barring unforeseen stardom, she was discussing her acting career with no one, nohow, period. What was the point of letting the world know you were on the verge of being a has-been would-be? Too humiliating. She continued to go to auditions at lunch because she had been doing it for years. Her hopes were weakened, but she didn't know how to stop trying to be an actress. It would mean trying to be something else, and there was nothing else she could think of being. She certainly didn't want to think of herself as a temporary legal secretary with a crush on a preoccupied lawyer. She noted to herself that Ernest had been less preoccupied lately. He seemed practically interested in her. But then, as she recalled the odds against her, she concluded that maybe she was wrong about that, too. More and more, as her birthday crept up, she was a member of the glumoisie.

Alors.

But, as that natural blonde, Loreli Lee, used to say, "Fate just keeps on happening."

On this fresh, fateful Wednesday morning, Lizzie mentions to Susan that perhaps they ought to have lunch in the park together. Susan says that that is a wonderful thought, but unfortunately, she made other plans days ago.

There are no auditions for Lizzie to go to today. It is two days before payday and Lizzie is too broke to go shopping. Ernie pokes his head out of his office door for no particular reason.

"What are you doing for lunch?" Lizzie asks him.

"Are you asking me to have lunch with you?"

wonders the generally intelligent fellow whose knees have just buckled beneath him.

Lizzie knows Ernest is a formal sort of guy. Now she's overstepped. "Well, you know. If you were going to get something to eat, I thought..."

Ernest looks toward Susan's partially opened door and places a finger to his lips. He retreats inside his office. Lizzie's day is ruined.

Ernest immediately picks up the telephone and dials Lizzie's extension. "Lizzie?"

"Is that you, Ernest?"

"Shh. Act natural. I want you to know I was thinking of asking you, but I thought it might be complicated."

"Evidently," whispers Lizzie.

"You understand, don't you?"

"No. I think you're nuts."

"Do you still want to have lunch?"

"Uh-huh."

"As soon as Susan leaves, we'll go."

Lizzie wonders if Ernest is dating Susan. Then matters would be complicated. "Do you want me to wear a trenchcoat?" she drawls.

In a hurry to protect his interest, for fear of the sudden evaporation of her interest, Ernest confesses before he can check himself. "It's just, frankly, Lizzie, I intend to be fully unprofessional about this."

Honesty begets honesty, and so Lizzie reassures him. "I feel the same way."

There is a heavy, moist silence.

"Well," says the manly take-charge Ernest, "if we're going to be unprofessional and get away with it, we have to be professional about it."

That Fateful Wednesday:
Part II

Marcy spent all last night tarnishing the metal surfaces in her apartment. After she had reupholstered her couch in a Scotchgarded Constitutional Parchment print, featuring the Bill of Rights on her throw pillows, she had been retro-moved by the fact that with all the money they had thrown around, the nabobs who had been responsible for the mega-hoopla had not spent a nickel to polish up the copper to gleaming copper-color for the Statue of Liberty's one hundredth birthday. This could mean only one thing, and Marcy had nearly overlooked it: Statue-of-Liberty green was very, very up-and-coming, and would soon be absolutely in. First she submitted her copper-bottomed pots to the searing flames of the gas burners on her stove. Then she bathed them in vinegar to achieve the desired verdigris. She placed her silverplated flatware and a treasured Victorian serving dish in lemon juice to soak overnight. The out-of-date sheen of the bronze-framed coffee table was easily muted with acetic acid, and, as she waited for the discoloration to

occur, she drifted to sleep on the couch, dreaming of pa-
tina.

The next morning, as she fixed her morning coffee,
she admired the blackened silverplate sitting in her sink.
She could not resist rubbing a little silver polish here and
there to accentuate the iridescent black with a blunted
sterling gray. Now her Fortunoff repros looked as though
they had been carried down from Ralph Lauren's imaginary great grandma's attic somewhere in the small, well-
decorated town of R. H. Macy's, Vermont. (Actually,
Marcy's Rumanian great grandma had lived all her adult
life in a second-floor Bronx apartment not five blocks
away from Mrs. Lifshitz, and had not been in an attic
since she hid from soldiers during the pogroms.)

Just as Marcy had the opportunity to create her own
heritage with a bit of acid and a credit card, so she was
now about to enhance her chances to create her own fate
with a trip to Love at First Sight.

When you have a product like love for sale, considerable attention must be paid to what it is. The Love at First
Sight company philosophy, according to the brochure
Marcy received when she took out a membership, is that
love should be fun, upscale, romantic, and disease-free.
All members of Love at First Sight sign a pledge that they
are unmarried and sincerely ready to share at least one
walk in the park with a remarkable single friend of the
opposite sex, selected from among the vast collection of
videos, prior to exercising the option to bid adieu. They
try to discourage the use of the word "reject." In order to
make a Love at First Sight personal video, members must
submit to a physical examination and an afternoon of free
single-image consulting. Marcy's health is fine, but she is
not yet ready to make a video of her own. She has opted
to view a maximum of five tapes during her introductory
two-month membership, so that she can check out the eli-

gible men while remaining discreetly invisible. If she chooses to date up to three of these five men, her obligations are minimal. Still, the costs and the stakes are high and she must choose carefully.

Love at First Sight is nothing if not atmosphere. As Marcy wheels her shopping cart down the candlelit aisles, her attention is drawn to the smoky spotlights illuminating each of the categories. She wheels quickly past the *Marrying Kind* cassettes, lingering to admire the sensuously carved cheekbones of this week's man featured in the *Unattainable Gods and Goddesses* section. She is tempted, but not at these prices. As a holographic image of Flagrante Delecto sings, "You may not be fifteen but you're still beautiful to me," Marcy glides past the *Latin Lovers* to the *Wealthy Playboys Who Are Looking for Something More* section of the store. She is not alone. In the flickering light Marcy can see three or four women eyeing the appealingly illuminated photographs on the covers of the videocassettes. The featured charmer, his ebony hair tousled to the perfect degree, has eyes as alluring as the Mona Lisa's and as meltingly world-weary as a basset hound. His lower lip juts in a pout that all but says the world of the international jet set is a bore without you. He is neither burly nor a pretty boy. He is a classic, all class in a class by himself.

While the other women gaze and dream, Marcy acts decisively. She takes the cassette from the shelf and walks directly to the checkout counter. Emerging victorious from the store, Marcy takes a moment to adjust to the bright daylight. She savors the thought of the women who are, at this moment, castigating themselves for letting *him* get away so easily.

Before Marcy tucks the video away in her black-and-white pony-skin duffel, she looks at the spine of the cassette jacket for the name of her prize. *Dick Judd.* There's a name Marcy can feel in her groin. She's just begun to put her plans into action. Marcy hails a taxi to take her to the fountain in front of the Plaza Hotel. Susan is a few minutes late, so Marcy distracts herself by watching a talented mime whose decidedly cute buns are accentuated by his leotard. Just as I recognize this fellow as Michael the Mime, Susan arrives and gives Marcy a peck on the cheek.

"Hi, Suze." Marcy doesn't take her eyes off Michael's performance. "Isn't that a tush you could die for?"

As Susan smiles, an amused hiss escapes her lips. She hopes that this will be sufficient response. Susan is not prone to graphic commentary.

Michael the Mime spots the new member of his audience. He more than spots her. He knows her to be the woman he selected to be the mother of his imaginary children. He positions himself in front of Susan and pulls up an imaginary seat. Susan is ablaze with embarrassment but decides it will be better to cooperate. As he gestures for her to sit in a seat across the imaginary table, she complies, to the delight of the rest of the audience. Michael the Mime then pops the imaginary cork of imaginary champagne, and pours Susan a glass. Michael's motions are so precise that Susan can visualize it: a gold-edged fluted glass with a delicate twisted stem. Michael pours one for himself. Twining his arm around hers, he nods a toast.

"Thank you," says Susan. Their eyes lock. Susan forgets that there are seventy-five onlookers. Michael takes a sip. Susan takes a sip. The applause of the crowd causes Susan's imaginary champagne to spill, and her concentration breaks. Marcy applauds with double zest. Susan offers her silent friend a handshake.

"You were terrific," he whispers. Then he winks. At Susan. And for the next half hour, Susan doesn't think about anything but her champagne cocktail companion. She doesn't hear a word Marcy says about Love at First Sight and the rest of her schedule.

The Significant Lunch

Ernest appreciates the happy happenstance of Lizzie's impulsive invitation but doesn't feel comfortable with it. He feels vaguely as if something has been taken out of his manly hands. In order to put the missing ingredient back into his hands, he has, unbeknownst to Lizzie, taken charge of the preparations with what might be called a vengeance.

They will not be going to Pizza Hut for a slice. No-a-saki!

"Where to?" asks the unsuspecting Lizzie.

Ernest won't answer. As the taxi whisks the twosome down Park Avenue, Ernest grins his newly acquired man-about-town grin. He will not make the mistakes he made with Marcy. Now that he has made partner, he feels more secure. He will risk fun-ness. Lizzie is game.

I understand, of course. But you know how I feel when a good damsel bites the dust. Not that Ernest is dust, but—she could do so much better. Ah, well . . . I will regard this amour as a detour on the road of love.

Lizzie recognizes the polished obsidian entryway from the photographs she's seen in *Architectural Digress*. Her mouth begins to water before they've passed through the famous portals. The most frequently used description of this restaurant is "indescribable." That about sums it up. Sushi Faggots from Hell is, after all, more than a restaurant; it is an environmental gustatory experience.

Lizzie had no idea that Ernest was the kind of man who would frequent such a place. But here she is. With him. They are greeted by a top-knotted former sumo wrestler wearing a black leather kimono. They remove their shoes and place monogrammed velvet slippers on their feet before being led to a private table for two. Without thinking, Lizzie reaches across the table and takes Ernest's hand. Then she thinks: *This one isn't going to get away.*

She lets Ernest order. They have the number 7 and the number 18, followed by the number 33 with jasmine tea and green tea ice cream. As the waiter carries each marble plate to the table, the entrée is highlighted by a discreet spotlight. Ernest rises from his seat, which is too far away from Lizzie, and slides beside her on the black leather cushions. They gaze at each other in a way that is only enchanting to the two of them and say very little, all in all.

Normally, Lizzie would have been very interested to know that as they dined, Barbra Streisand, the noted cosmetic surgeon Dr. Blatt and his old wife with her newest nose, two of Isabella Rossellini's former lovers, and their respective former lovers all dined nearby. But at the moment she is thinking of only one thing: How very sexy an overworked, repressed lawyer might turn out to be.

It goes without saying that Lizzie's newfound happiness is my happiness as well. But let's talk about something else, darlings.

After lunch the two travel separately by taxi to W, P & H, taking special care to enter the office separately, and several minutes apart. All this is for nought. Susan isn't there to notice.

Marcy Eats Light
But Continues to Grow

Marcy tries criticizing—"You have to take personal responsibility for your personal life"—and cajoling —"Please please pretty please, I can't stand to go to this kind of thing by my self. I'll be your best friend"—but neither works on Susan. As they munch on an expensive pile of miniature green vegetables, Marcy's mind wanders in the direction of the great unknown and unlimited romantic possibilities of the new technologies, and Susan's thoughts continue to linger in front of the Plaza Hotel fountain. Marcy resigns herself to attending the Personal Growth Class alone.

Marcy welcomes every opportunity to improve herself with holy zest. She favors the wide approach, a course here, a seminar there; some for the body, some for the soul. Once every two or three years she repeats the first few lessons of the intermediate French course at Alliance Français, but she never finishes. Something always interrupts. Finishing isn't the point for Marcy; *movement* is— that fine sense of doing something. She has a hard time tolerating stagnation for even a week. When Ernest used to blob out, she panicked. And when she panicked, she *did* something. She is afraid that she will grow roots in her fit bottom, that her underarm skin will begin to flap, and that one day she will wake up to find that she has turned into her listless mother. Marcy is, in her own way, quite well educated. All those half-completed courses put her on speaking terms with just about any subject that doesn't involve math.

Marcy has decided not to take notes today. She just sits in the front row, listening closely.

She has never seen a woman as bubbly as Bev, her Personal Growth instructor. Dressed in pink jogging clothes, this bouncy woman enthuses so vigorously that Marcy begins to feel old and tired.

"For those of you who missed my workshops on How to Flirt, How to Get a First Date, and Grinning, Bearing, Sharing, and Caring, or What to Do with Someone after You've Had a First Date, the important thing is to let your own personal beauty shine through. But, and I repeat, but, do not get too personal too soon. It's intimidating. And the name of the game is intimacy, not intimidation."

Bev pitter-patters over to the blackboard. She writes:

Intimacy = YES!!!!!!!
Intimidation = NO*&#$@!!!!

and then asks, "Any questions?"

Marcy looks around the room. There are eight women and two men, all of whom indicate that they do not question Bev. She likes that.

"Try an opening gambit which allows the playful spirit of your personal flirtatiousness to shine through. You can do this anywhere." She returns to the blackboard to write out every word she has just said. "At the store. On a bus . . . any other ideas?"

A man with roseate acne raises his left hand while

covering the lower half of his face with his right. "In the office?" he asks. He has a very handsome voice.

"Never in the office. That's sexual harassment. If you'd like to learn more about that, take my workshop on Sexual Harassment—Do's, Don't's, and How to Get Around Them. Any other ideas?"

Bev has intimidated the class. No one raises so much as an eyebrow. Bev is undeterred. She speaks in capital letters, knowing what she has to say will be important to those who are ready to understand it.

"Let's move on to Assertiveness. In order to pick someone up—we will call this making primary emotional contact—you must speak. First. You may have the opportunity to catch his or her eye, but the next move separates the men from the sheep. Shy away, and you may be relegated to the back pastures of happiness. Speak up, seize the moment, and you will be able to actualize your personal interactive potential in every way each and every day. So speak up!! Take control of making the first move."

Bev furrows her bouncy brow. She sees no reason why everyone in the room should not be totally actualized.

"You gotta stay in there and keep punching if you wanna win. Love is war. Love is entrepreneurial. Love means being able to be vulnerable, but if you want to be vulnerable and win, don't let your weak spots show. Remember, someone out there who is more perfect than you may be vying for your future mate. You have to stay on top of things all the time. And if the mate you have seems under par, move on. Single women, check out the husbands of your married friends. If they can't keep their husbands, then maybe you can. The main point is, know what you want and go after it. If you don't know what you want—pretend you do. And go after that. If you wait for someone else to start the game of love, if you linger and languish and wait for some knight on a white horse to make a move—you may be destined to a life of lonely wimpitude and you will have only your unactualized self to blame. You may wait *forever*."

Oh, were I less discreet or valorous, the things I could tell you about Bev. Forgive me this outburst, but she causes my princely testicles to shrivel. Even I, who have only love to give, have enemies.

Somehow Work Seems
to Have Taken
a Backseat

       After lunch, Susan takes the roundabout route so that she might pass the Plaza Hotel on her way back to the office. Michael the Mime is gone, as is the crowd he attracted. Susan doesn't admit that she had hoped not only to see him again, but to somehow speak to him, maybe know him a little bit. She says to herself that she was just curious. And anyway, what difference would it make if she did see him again? She crosses the street and gazes into the windows of Bergdorf Goodman, taking in the cabbage-headed models and their rose jersey princess dresses. Susan remembers that when she was a young girl whose body was essentially tubular, one day her mother spoke to her in a new and casual way. She said, "You'll have a figure like mine. Wear princess dresses, they cover a multitude of sins." Then she giggled. Susan meant to take this particular advice, because it was not offered in a maternal way, but friend to friend. It was the first time she thought of her mother as having a figure at all. Later that day, Susan and her mother had had a cup of coffee together at the St. Moritz, Susan's first restaurant cup of coffee, and dessert without lunch. By the time Susan was old enough to have a figure, princess dresses had vanished from the stores, and she covered her multitude of uncommitted sins with gabardine suiting. Susan figures that this princess dress costs a king's ransom, so she drifts on.

Somehow she finds herself sitting behind her desk, staring out her window replaying approximately four minutes of her afternoon over and over, embellishing them, adding different endings to the scene she had hoped to find waiting for her by the fountain.

Lizzie is thumbing through a *Vogue*, and wondering how she can lose five pounds before tonight.

Ernest is doing his best to be preoccupied only with Lizzie, and would like to feel arousal at the thought of her. However, he is trapped by a reflex as involuntary as breathing: He buries his sensual reveries under his work. At no time does Ernest abandon his responsibilities. This is his gravest fault and his finest quality.

In Which
Marcy Actualizes

Spurred by Bev's exhortation, Marcy's responsibility is to further actualize herself at the earliest possible opportunity. For this reason—with only a brief stopover to acquire an ostrich handbag guaranteed to give her the aura of a deposed monarch's daughter or your money back—she is at the men's clothing department of the expensively redecorated Barney's admiring the sea island cotton–and–silk blend sports shirts in front of her. Seeing a perfectly groomed man who appears to be worthy of her, she picks up a salmon-and-mustard-striped item.

She approaches her prey. "Excuse me," she says oh so sweetly, "I'm picking out a shirt for my brother. Do you mind if I hold it up against your body to see how it would look?"

"Be my guest," quoth the prey.

Pressing the garment to his torso, smoothing it and his chest with her hands, she strokes upward toward his shoulders and steps back to admire. "That looks terrific! The shade is just perfect!"

"Let me see."

Still holding the shirt to his chest, Marcy leads her prey over to a full-length mirror.

"Very becoming," she says.

"Yes, it is nice. You have excellent taste."

Marcy sighs. "Why, thank you."

"Your lucky brother. I wonder if there are any more in this color combination."

They hurry back to the counter together and begin rifling through the remaining shirts for a match. It seems there are no more salmon mustards, and since Marcy does not really have a brother, she decides to give him the one she is holding under false pretenses. "My brother won't know the difference. I'll just get another stripe."

The prey accepts her gesture. "You are very kind. I was looking for a present for my boyfriend. It's our anniversary. And this is just the thing to go with his new Versace."

"Oh, perfect," growls Marcy. She should have known he was too well groomed to be heterosexual. She's lived in the city for years.

She doesn't want to give up, nor does she want to go aground on her lucky day. She contemplates a change of venue. She doesn't want the type who goes for sports equipment—too vain. Maybe electronics. No. She thinks people who talk about computers are even more boring than people who go on about Cuisinart blades. She's at a loss, when all of a sudden—pling!—David Hightest, Ellis Yuppington's analyst, appears at the end of her aisle. And boy is he cute and boy is he ripe for the proverbial picking.

There is nothing I can do to stop any of this. Marcy is on a roll.

Seeing nothing but a physically perfect specimen of what God had in mind when he created Man, the entranced Marcy grabs the nearest garment and hurries to be near the object of her desire.

"Hi. I'm picking out a shirt for my brother. Do you mind if I hold it up against you to see how it would look?"

With more confidence than any one man deserves, David inspects this frosted blonde with the cute little dimple in one cheek. "Those look like slacks to me."

"Well heavenly bejesus," mutters Marcy, as she looks at what are indeed a pair of corduroy pants clutched in her well-manicured mitts, "you're so right."

David's shoulders square, and his eyes flash just like a romantic hero in one of Marcy's Harlequins, as her heart leaps into her throat just like it would were she a romantic heroine. Suddenly there seems to be a hair-tousling breeze that smells faintly of purple heather.

Marcy politely clears her throat. "What is your name?"

"David."

"I'm Marcy."

"Nice to meet you, Marcy. Want me to show you the difference between a shirt and a pair of trousers?"

"At my place?" she asks boldly.

Each, as a responsible adult, is aware of the possibilities for catching grabby little viruses through anonymous sexual encounters, so they stop for a quick blood test before heading uptown.

Hers and Mime

Michael the Mime cleans up at lunchtime, grossing and netting—they're the same thing to him—close to five hundred dollars for three hours' work. And he gets a look at that woman again. What is it about her? She isn't one of those impenetrable tootsies who have it all and don't need anything they can't give themselves. Nor is she the trembling painter-of-miniature - pet - portraits - who - doesn't - think - she - should - be - the-one-to-put-food-on-the-table type. Not at all. Susan falls into the Professional Woman category, but Michael, whose observation antennae are the tools of his trade, senses appealing trace elements of the Amateur Woman about her. He intuits that she is ready to take a chance because she is clearly missing something he can happily provide: enchantment.

Now Michael has a mission. He needs to be loved by a woman he enchants, by a woman who has the qualities he lacks and lacks the qualities he has—especially with the cold weather approaching and the prospect of a winter of being enchanted alone.

He puts out the word among his street friends to find out where she works and has an answer within the hour. The rest is up to him. Michael buys two fluted goblets from Tiffany's. He purchases a chilled bottle of Mumm's and has it packed in ice. He stops at the Polish Tea Room in the Edison Hotel for caviar blinis-to-go. At 4:40 he positions himself outside the revolving doors of Witkin, Pritkin & Harris headquarters.

He is worried that the woman he wishes to entertain won't recognize him without his makeup, so he sets his treasures on the sidewalk and applies his white disguise.

Michael doesn't have to wait long, because the unsuspecting Susan has been clock-watching all afternoon. Now it is 4:41. Now it is 4:43. Susan, who is accustomed to staying very, very late, is trying to concoct a valid excuse for leaving early and the thought of staying within her allotted four walls for a respectable fifteen minutes is almost unbearable. She doesn't understand it. She checks her Filofax. Maybe it's premenstrual syndrome. No. Two weeks to p-day. It must be another syndrome. There has to be an explanation.

Rising from her chair she says, "Oh, good lord! I forgot completely about it!" for the benefit of Lizzie. Lizzie pays no attention. Susan packs up her briefcase and wrangles her elbows into her coat. Affecting all the briskness of a woman with a purpose, she shuts her office door behind her and approaches the secretarial desk. "I'm going out. I'll be at the Columbia Law Library, where I can't be reached. If Ernest wants to get hold of me, have him leave a message with my machine at home. If anyone else needs me . . . well, I'm not expecting any emergencies. Anyway, I'm out the door."

"Have a nice time," says Lizzie.

"What do you mean by that?" Susan ricochets, thinking that Lizzie suspects her delinquency.

"Nothing," answers Lizzie dreamily. She's already forgotten what she said.

Susan meets Honoroff in the elevator and feels the need to offer an even more elaborate explanation for her defection. She tells him she plans to pull an all-nighter doing research for the firm. This earns her praise from the big H himself and an escort out the revolving door.

Susan would not have deduced that the man with the champagne bucket was waiting for her—except in her private and recently uncontrollable fantasies—had he not a dead-white face, and lips that formed the silent word, "You." Now she has figured out that she is the "you" to whom he refers and she cannot let him leave without her because miracles do not happen twice. Honoroff rattles on about—what? Susan can't claim to be listening. She is desperate.

"Oh!" she exclaims. "You'll have to excuse me, Mr. Honoroff, but I completely forgot my, uh, briefcase upstairs!"

"You have your briefcase in your hand," he observes with all the exactitude of a seasoned legal professional.

"That's just it!" she recoups. "I accidentally picked up Ernest Barnes's briefcase in my hurry."

"Would you like me to wait? We can take a cab up together."

"No. No, that's very kind. I don't want to hold you up. We'll continue our conversation tomorrow."

"It's no trouble," he persists.

"No, no, no. You're *too* kind!" She dashes back in the revolving doors before Honoroff can be any kinder. She scuttles past the elevators to the newsstand at the back exit.

Suddenly she has a horrible thought. What if she imagined the mime? What if he wasn't really there at all? She buys a chocolate-covered cherry, counts to ten, then retraces her scuttles back from whence she came.

He's still there. He applauds. "Well done."

"Thank you," she says. "What are you doing here?"

"You were so good at drinking imaginary champagne, I thought you'd like some of the real thing."

"Well..." Susan scouts the territory for embarrassment potential, but sees no one she knows. She doesn't know this mime, either. Maybe she shouldn't do this. Why is she even considering prancing along the city streets with a man who wears foundation? Maybe he's a mass murderer. "Yes, I'd love to, I guess. But—not here."

"In case someone should see you?"

"How did you find me?"

"Where to?"

"You're the street type. Find us a street."

And so he does. Until an irritable police officer who has not given his quota of parking tickets threatens to arrest the two of them for drinking in public. Then Susan finds herself on the rooftop of a turn-of-the-century Brooklyn row house, gazing at that chic green emblem of Franco-American friendship and asking herself no questions as she huddles under the mime's jacket for warmth, and tissues off his makeup to see what she's really gotten into.

By 6:15, Ernest and Lizzie have left the office separately together, Marcy and David Hightest have settled onto Marcy's couch to share a snifter of Armagnac, and Susan and Michael the Mime have exchanged names and the occasional kiss.

Crescendo

At the Ava von Hollywood concert for which Ernest has managed to wangle scalper tickets, as the crowd rocks on its collective feet, as Lizzie's rapt attention is only upon the man in whose arms she is wrapped, *she thinks she is with me.* As Susan watches moonlight paint the ships in New York Harbor aided by the light of an earthly torch, as she relishes the jolt of Michael's kisses on her neck, *she thinks she is with me.* Only dear Marcy has no illusions about the company she keeps. That, too, is a good thing. At least she doesn't mistake that chiseled-chinned so-and-so for me.

Despite the cases of mistaken identity, at least Lizzie and Susan are with me in spirit. To put it another way, I doubt that Ernest and Michael would be enjoying their favors were there not some confusion about who was and was not Prince Charming. And as for Marcy, though she prefers to think that true love is just the name of fifteen songs and a magazine or two, she'll come around when the time is right.

* * *

And so:

While David unbuttons Marcy's jumpsuit, Michael suggests that he and Susan go indoors. As Susan's tour of the Victorian oak details in Michael's apartment terminates in the bedroom with a view of the elaborately stamped tin ceiling, Marcy slides between her ready and waiting peach satin sheets, pulling David down beside her. As Ava von Hollywood sings an explosive ballad of lust, Ernest and Lizzie hold hands. Ernest brushes a stray lock of hair from Lizzie's eyes as Marcy runs her hands across David's silky chest. Susan is terrified and wonders if she is drunk as she pulls herself back up into a sitting position on the edge of Michael's futon. He gently kneels beside her and removes her shoes, then her stockings. Susan is secretly pleased she is wearing thigh highs and a red lacy garter belt instead of the usual beige-tone pantyhose. Michael is openly surprised; Susan doesn't seem the type. But the type that doesn't seem the type is often the best type. David earnestly raises himself on his arms to look at his new lover. (He is not earnest, just practiced.) Marcy averts her eyes. Then she closes them and turns her mouth toward David's as he plunges himself deep inside her. Feeling shy, Susan turns out the light. Michael protests. He wants to see her. Susan promises that there will be another time. And then, as Michael caresses her as if he has known her body for years, she is certain that there will be time after time after time. He pulls her onto his lap, as she urges him toward abandon. Then she stops, suddenly, to let the passion intensify. Susan thought she had forgotten the ways of love, but it's like riding a bicycle. Lizzie discovers that Ernest's earlobes have a direct line to his lower brain, and she coaxes his train of thought until the concert is over. The late supper plans are forgotten in their urgency, and the rapid consummation of their desires seems a certainty until Lizzie tells the taxi driver to take them to Blackwatch Towers. A wave of panic disguised as rationality drowns Ernest's arousal as he recognizes the address of his ex. He does not want to go to Blackwatch, not now. Nor does he want to explain why. So he redirects the cab to an all-night diner. The turnabout comes so suddenly that Lizzie cannot even manage to ask why. But over coffee and buttered rye toast, Ernest comes up with an excuse that will serve as an honorable truth: They have something so special that it cannot be rushed. He is dying to make love to her, but their blossoming love is meant to be more than a collision of bodies, and so they must wait until the time is right. Lizzie is even more certain that she has found me, her Prince Charming, when she hears his reasons for holding back. Never mind that they are half-false. Susan, too, becomes more certain that Michael is Prince Charming as years of inhibition fall away. Lovemaking with Michael is the easiest thing she has ever done. And the best. She could live for this, she thinks at a moment when thinking is almost impossible, and she has not yet arrived at the evening's ultimate pleasure. Ernest's good-night kiss manages to convey the promise of hotter things to come. At home, each one alone, neither Ernest nor Lizzie can resist privately imagining the pleasures they have chosen not yet to share. The imagination evokes irresistible sensations which cannot wait for satiation. Although he is alone in his apartment, Ernest closes the bathroom door behind him. Lizzie steps into a hot bath. Marcy clutches David's back. Susan's emotions come loose in tears she cannot stifle as both David and Michael cry out, "I love you," and mean completely different things by it.

At any rate, everybody comes. All at the same time. Magnificently. Everybody except me.

The Post-Coital Report

Bartlett's *Familiar Quotations* is full of remarks about love. And as far as the dictionary is concerned, love means everything from searing sexual desire to zero. I see no need to provide you with a pithy quote about love as I embark on my post-coital analysis. We know what we mean.

After changing his sheets (for no related reason) and crawling between them, Ernest telephones Lizzie. "I just wanted to say good-night," he whispers, and then they talk for half an hour more until neither feels like sleeping. Lizzie goes to the medicine cabinet and finds her tryptophan. She takes two with a glass of milk. After that infusion of amino acids, not even love can keep her awake. As she sleeps, she dreams of me, erotically, I might add. I might also add that in these dreams, I seem to bear a disturbing resemblance to a corporate lawyer.

Michael the Mime sleeps sweetly, holding Susan with a dead man's grip. She is wide awake. She cannot move. She boldly studies Michael's face. His curling lashes, the trace of clown white under his chin, the hairs in his nose. He must be about thirty, she figures, maybe younger. And a mime. She wonders what he *really* does, because she cannot imagine anyone but Marcel Marceau actually miming for a living. She rehearses what she might say about this Michael who makes love so beautifully. "I'd like you to meet my friend"—too vague, "boyfriend"—too teenage, "my lover"—too frank, "my fiancé"—too soon, never would be too soon: How could I marry a mime? What would I tell people? I'd like you to meet Michael. He's in miming. Not mining. He's a mime. A mimist. A mimeticist. At any rate, he's not a lawyer. Michael adjusts his position. Without awakening, he kisses her shoulder. Susan cannot easily recall the last time she slept with another human being. She's not comfortable lying on someone else's sheets. If she had to do it every day, she would be a very tired woman. She cannot imagine growing used to another body's presence. When dreaming of marriage, she had not considered this aspect. She wriggles free, and wakes Michael in the process. "I can't sleep. I'm going home to my bed."

"No," he grumbles. "Stay." She means to kiss him good-bye, but he makes love to her again. And then she goes into the night alone.

Marcy regards David Hightest as he slithers out of bed.

"And now for some post-coital pleasantry," says David as he positions his pants leg for entry.

"And some witty rejoinder," Marcy rejoins.

"I'll call you soon."

"That's not witty. You want something to eat? I'm a professional."

Almost involuntarily, David pats his pocket to assure himself that he still has his wallet. "A professional?"

Marcy hears the anxiety in his voice. "Caterer, darling. Do I look like a hooker?"

"Without clothes, everyone looks the same. Besides, I don't make value judgments."

Marcy hasn't heard that phrase in years. "What's that supposed to mean?"

"It's a catch-all for avoiding the commitment involved in making a definite statement, and a way to put the listener at ease. Anyway, I'd better be going. You were great though."

"Isn't that a value judgment?"

"How does that make you feel?"

"I feel like you talk funny. But I like you. Anyway, how come you have to go home?"

"Umm...all-night things are no good for me. I have a difficult schedule," he says in a significant tone.

Marcy has heard this significant tone in the movies, so she knows her next line. "There's someone else?"

"Umm...yes," David hesitates. He needs a moment to suss out her reaction to this confession and whether it will involve tears or worse. He knows a man in his position can rarely escape without a to-do. Sneaking a glance at his watch, he braces himself for whatever comes, as long as it doesn't last more than half an hour.

But he doesn't know Marcy.

She jumps up on the bed like a gleeful seven-year-old. "Really?!" she giggles. "You mean I'm an Other Woman? Wow! On my first go-round. Wow! Furtive meetings. Guilty sex. And my evenings free!"

Marcy is so excited that even after David Hightest makes his quick, happy, but baffled exit, she forgets to look at the Love at First Sight video buried at the bottom of her discarded pony-skin satchel.

Visible Side Effects

In the days that follow, certain patterns are established:

1. Ernest can be seen reading *Interview* and *Spy* and *Tatler* and *Details* and *Sins of Omission* in addition to *The New York Times* and the *New England Journal of Law.* He is determined not to be dull. He purchases a hand-painted silk tie and actually wears it to work. He is stopped by the same security guard who has seen him day after day, year after year, and asked for identification proving that he works at Witkin, Pritkin & Harris. Ernest's reaction to this affront is to buy a similar hand-painted tie in another color. And wear a pink shirt. Lest you think the man has abandoned all caution, I remind you that Brooks Brothers sells a very suitable pink shirt, with a choice of either button or French cuffs.

2. Lizzie comes to work tired. She has been going out every night to newer and trendier clubs. She had no idea that Ernest was so resourceful. Last night they tried to get into Swell's, the quintessentially chic nightclub. Even Marcy has not been to Swell's, not that you can actually go there. The location, which changes every two weeks, is

unannounced and fashionably unmarked. In addition, the door policy is to turn away celebrity and riffraff alike unless the applicant possesses the secretly determined *je ne sais quoi*, which is freshly *sais*ed and *quoi*ed behind Pinkerton-guarded doors each afternoon. If you don't have it, forget it. With hundreds of other stylish couples, Ernest and Lizzie waited an hour and a half on the roped-off line until they were rejected by the bouncers. There was no anger or embarrassment involved. They were in the *very* best of company. Aroused by the chill in the night air, they happily hurried back to Ernest's apartment for a bout of heavy petting. Each night, Ernest and Lizzie find themselves together in his apartment. He doesn't seem to want to go to hers. *Technically*, they have not yet made love. They are officially "getting to know each other." As a result of this restraint, they find each other exceptionally stimulating. Lizzie has been reading a great deal about women reclaiming the right to say no, and she feels she is on the cutting edge of this trend. However, she did expect to have a little less cooperation from Ernest. She supposes that his reserve means that he truly respects her, and doesn't yet trust her to be germ-free. She feels ever so slightly rejected as a result of his moderation, but they are trying to build a relationship built on trust from the start, so she doesn't bring the matter up. At work, Ernest and Lizzie are more formal with each other than they were before. They do not leave together, even for lunch. They do not meet in the neighborhood. And no one catches on. Lizzie starts wearing a trenchcoat. It is a private joke.

3. Susan has come to expect surprises. Michael the Mime is unpredictable in a devoted sort of way. On Monday he messengered a sack full of tiger-eye marbles to her office but didn't call. She didn't see him Tuesday, but Wednesday he telephoned her at home and asked her to meet him in front of the big clock in Grand Central Terminal Thursday

morning at 7:00 A.M. She did. He arrived in full makeup and costume. "I work the rush hours," he explained, "but I thought we could have breakfast." This they did, in the stationmaster's office. Michael the Mime knows the stationmaster, not to mention a lot of other unlikely people. Susan introduced herself by first name only. She didn't really want the stationmaster to know who she was. Susan wishes she didn't embarrass so easily. It makes her feel so un-funloving, when in fact she's never had so much fun. Michael and she made love in an oak-paneled secret room adjacent to the inbound tracks under the station. Susan fully expected to see alligators crawling along the damp ground. When she climaxed—and Michael made a point of seeing that she did—she felt the earth move. The 8:15 from Stamford was on time. Susan was in the office only slightly later than usual. Ernest and Lizzie have both noticed how relaxed she seems lately. Ernest jokingly suggested to Lizzie that maybe Susan was having a hot affair. Lizzie laughed. They both think they know Susan better than that. Susan knows she has a secret. That, too, is fun. She goes around feeling sexy at the most unlikely times. During boring meetings, she treats herself to toasty reveries. Thank heaven, she thinks during one inappropriately timed mental rerun, women don't get erections.

4. Marcy is new at this, but already she's had a few thoughts on the ways that being an Other Woman is different from being the same woman she was. For one, there is the matter of the man. Ernest was just too, let's face it, vertical, while her entanglement with David Hightest seems to be entirely horizontal. As you know, any Prince Charming worth your golden slipper rotates on an 180-degree axis, twenty-four hours a day. Marcy isn't ready for that.

Marcy is consumed by speculation about the Other Other Woman who may or may not be David Hightest's wife. David is reluctant to talk about what he calls his "personal arrangements." He is a psychiatrist, so he cannot talk about his work. When she talks about herself,

Marcy has the feeling David understands her. What she doesn't like is the suspicion that he may be probing to uncover her weaknesses, out of a sort of professional habit. When he says, "How do you feel about that?" she wants to tell him, but then she defiantly reminds herself how little he is prepared to tell her.

She has decided that the root of the word *mistress* is *mystery*. She doesn't want to give herself away. For this reason, all they ever have is fun. Conversation is limited to food, movies, world events, and flirtatious banter.

This leaves plenty of time for sex.

Marcy has further decided that when and if they go out, he should pay for everything because she is the mistress and must regard all that he lavishes upon her as a down payment for the future trouble he will inevitably bring, either in the process of getting rid of her competition or not getting rid of it.

The vague film of dissatisfaction over Marcy's life has been refined into a super-charged sheen of craving.

Having entered the realm of mistressdom, Marcy now answers the door wearing nothing but a mink coat. There is always a bottle of champagne chilling in the fridge. She invests in dozens of silk nothings with elaborate lace trimmings. She buys herself red split-crotch eat-away panties—though she hasn't had the nerve to wear them because she thinks David might think that she has psychological quirks. Marcy no longer complains about anything. At least not to David. She doesn't want to be a nag. She pretends to be understanding if David cancels a rendezvous at the last minute. She tries to be everything she fancies the Other Other isn't. It takes her mind off other other *other* things.

Marcy has gained five pounds in as many days.

Ellis Yuppington Plans
to Effectively Drop
the *Y* in His Name

Magenta Smarm, Ellis Yuppington's pert assistant, would not permit a copy of *People* to smudge her manicured hands, but she is a voracious reader of *Vanity Fair*, and has made it her business to get to know a cousin of the associate style editor. Through this cousin, she met the associate style editor, himself, and made a point of letting him know how charming she could be.

As Thanksgiving approaches, and with it the season of holiday galas, Magenta Smarm advises Ellis of the increase in opportunities for mending an unsightly bump on his visibility profile while creating, shall we say, not just a social splash, but a veritable, and discreet social tsunami.

Thanksgiving is, for most Americans, a family affair. But what about the aristotrash, Eurocrats, and those neglected scions of the Great Houses of Europe, past and present, British and exotic, who, for one reason or another, cannot be with their own while their kith are with kin? Are these disenfranchised Royals to be denied their fair share of cranberry sauce simply because they don't have the right heritage? Imagine the need Ellis Yuppington can fill.

Handsome, charming, youthful, successful entrepreneurs are a dime on the dollar a dozen these days. Magenta knows Ellis needs something more than that to distinguish himself as a worthy host.

It is no secret that Ellis suffers from B-list stagnation. One look at the haunted pallor lingering under his tanned complexion tells you that when King Juan Carlos throws a bash in Majorca, Ellis stays home. Ellis could afford to take himself to Majorca, but that is hardly the point. Without a transfusion of old blood into his personal life, Ellis is doomed to drift; undetected cosmic dust in the social firmament. He needs a countess he can count on, a duke with whom to be seen.

Magenta, who has just this morning come directly from the arms of an informed source, has determined that there is an opportunity to use what influence she has developed to get Ellis into the "Best Parties You Could Not Possibly Be Invited To" column. This will do the trick. She would not ordinarily call in a favor to help someone other than herself, and this is no exception. Magenta plans to use Yuppington's party to launch her own new subcareer as a celebutante. She can already imagine herself in her fanciful toque, monopolizing the photo on the glossy page. All Ellis has to do is cooperate—which, after she points out the social and possibly even tax advantages, he will.

Magenta sets to researching lonely aristocrats and leading jewelry and fashion designers who plan to be far from the family castle on Thanksgiving Day.

Ellis telephones Marcy, his Individual Culinary Image Consultant, and sets up an appointment to discuss the possibilities at the Post-Nuclear Bar at eight the next evening.

Meanwhile

Marcy sets to refining the concept as only she can. Her considerable talents are sharpened by the need to make the project interesting enough so that she can concentrate on something other than her preoccupying interest in what David Hightest does when he isn't doing something with her, and what whatever that is means *about* her.

With practiced professionalism, Marcy brushes aside the Thanksgiving notion. Though she shows promise, Magenta lacks the kind of understanding that comes from experience. Aristos, for one, do not like to be reminded by non-family members that they have things to be thankful for. Besides, Thanksgiving will be unseasonal in a December or January issue. Ellis will end up in the circular file, and henceforth the editors will associate him with the discardoisie. Christmas coverage will be ultracompetitive. Ellis needs something compelling, irresistible, timeless, new, and now.

Marcy pops an Advil and waits for the muse.

*　*　*

Last night Ernest had his first tiff, really a tifflet, with Lizzie about why he never wanted to come to her place and she always came to his.

"My place is bigger," he argued.

"How do you know," she had wisely answered, "if you have never seen my place?"

"What are you, a lawyer?" he snapped.

"Why? You have something against lawyers? Anything I should know?" she retorted.

Ernest realized that under other circumstances, spending time at his new love's flat would have been an entirely reasonable thing to do. But the matter of his new love living almost directly under his ex gave him palpitations of a Type A nature. What if Julio recognized him? What if there was a fire drill and all the inhabitants of the building were evacuated to the lobby? What if Susan spotted them?

"What if Susan spotted us?"

"What do you mean what if Susan spotted us?"

"She lives somewhere in your building."

"Blackwatch Towers?" Lizzie was genuinely surprised. "And what were you doing in Susan's apartment?"

"I wasn't in Susan's apartment. Or I haven't been recently." Recently is a subjective adverb. "And what difference would that make? You can't think—"

"I'm sorry." Lizzie put her arms around Ernest's neck and kissed his stubble. "That was silly of me. I guess I've got a little PMS. You know? I'm sorry."

"That's okay, you redhead."

Ernest relaxed, thinking the quibble had been laid to rest.

"Ernie," said Lizzie after having had some time to think, "someday, I hope Susan will have to find out about us. And besides, if, in all the time I have been living in Blackwatch Towers I have never seen her either coming or going, the odds of your doing so are nillish, are they not? And besides," she said, drawing on her hundreds of dollars' worth of instruction in the Lee Strasberg/Stanislavsky Method as tears flooded her eyes, "I feel like you don't really want to get to know me if you won't risk coming to my apartment. It makes me feel like you're hiding something or something."

Ernest had not wanted Lizzie to think he was hiding something, so he agreed to take his chances and come for take-out Chinese.

Having scored her historically important victory, Lizzie is left to ponder the consequences on an otherwise pleasant afternoon.

Fighting the War
After Winning the Battle

      The problem is the apartment. Lizzie lives alone in a clean, attractive building in a safe neighborhood with access to public transportation. Such luxury does not come cheap. She has made in this, as in many other aspects of her life, considerable sacrifices. She does not have a couch. She uses an old TV tray for her dining-room table. She has one chair with four working legs. She has outré pillows on the floor. She has favorite postcards and photos stuck into the frame of her mirror, one juice glass, and four antique cups and saucers, none of which match. And a twin-sized futon that doubles as the second chair.

      Lizzie treasures her antique silver hairbrush, with its pale yellow boar bristles, because it is the only object she owns that suits her real self exactly. Her makeshift house-hold furnishings were temporary, to be unnoticed like the furniture in a highway rest stop, having nothing to do with who she really is or where she is going, which is supposed to be somewhere else entirely. She didn't want to decorate and make do, she wanted to arrive.

Now her whole self-image is at stake. She doesn't want Ernest to have the impression her place will undoubtedly give him. She also does not want to tell Ernest of her struggles to become an actress in more than name only, because that is downbeat. And she wants to be upbeat, which is the way her real self would be if it had a chance. What this means, in practical terms, is that she must entirely refurnish and redecorate her apartment by around eightish.

She buzzes Ernest on the intercom. "Can we reschedule your evening appointment to about nine-thirty?"

"That's kind of late..." he answers hesitantly.

"The client, uh, has to take care of a few matters before he can meet."

"Mmm. Okay. But I'm hoping it will be a productive meeting."

"How productive?" asks Lizzie in her sultriest Kathleen Turner voice.

"You sound just like Kathleen Turner. You should be an actress," comments Susan as she wanders toward Lizzie's desk with a donut in her hand.

Lizzie hangs up the telephone and smiles a radiant actress smile at Susan. "Susan? Can we talk for a moment? In your office?"

"Sure," says Susan between chews.

Only the Names
and Gewgaws
Have Been Changed

Lizzie closes the office door behind her. Susan motions toward a chair, but Lizzie continues to pace.

"Do you know we live in the same building?" says Lizzie.

"We do?"

"Yup. Uh-huh. I'm second floor. Blackwatch Towers."

"No kidding."

"I'm absolutely serious. Ernest Barnes mentioned it in passing. Quite a coincidence."

"Yeah. We should maybe have coffee sometime."

"Or do laundry or something."

Susan begins to laugh as the agitated Lizzie twirls her hair.

"I have an *enormous* favor to ask you which I would ordinarily never ask you except that I'm a wreck. I met this wonderful guy and I invited him to dinner tonight."

"That's awful," Susan titters.

"Well, it's just that he's so . . . nice."

"That *can* be a problem."

Susan likes the idea of being taken into Lizzie's confidence. She has never felt particularly comfortable confiding in people herself, at least not when it comes to personal matters. Maybe, she thinks, that is because she rarely has personal matters to discuss, unless you consider career moves personal. Susan has an urge to do some girl-talking now, but she doesn't know how to plunge in. She's all but vibrating with the desire to talk about her situation—she prefers, for the sake of her nerves, to think of it as a situation rather than an affair—with Michael. She's tried to reach Marcy, whose expertise in mansmanship certainly surpasses her own, but Marcy has not returned her calls. Peculiar. She wonders if she dares to confide in Lizzie. But if she did, where would she start? Meanwhile, Lizzie is confiding in her. Susan figures that she can get the gist of womanly tête-à-tête-ing if she pays close attention. "Is he inappropriate?" she asks.

"Oh, no. He's so appropriate that I'm worried. I want to make the right impression." Lizzie mangles her hair so intensely that she almost forgets to continue.

Susan nods encouragingly.

Remembering her mission, Lizzie explains her predicament to the one person she thinks can help her. She vividly describes a German blond athlete with ruddy cheeks and bulging triceps, assigns him a career in business, which is a vague enough cover-all not to be an all-out lie, and otherwise fudges the details of her courtship with Ernest—who is darkish and basically bulges only when sexually aroused—so that Susan cannot suspect that the man in question is none other than her colleague. It would not do to have Susan relate the story to Ernest as an amusing anecdote, so Lizzie swears Susan to secrecy. Susan not only takes the oath in stride, but offers to aid, abet, and loan Lizzie her apartment for the evening. She volunteers to sleep on Lizzie's twin futon.

It's all settled until Lizzie knocks on Ernest's office

door. The real Lizzie would never deceive him this way. The temporary Lizzie soothes her ambivalence with some nifty reasoning about how, although she ought to be *unashamed* of who she is, and *ashamed* of what she is doing, she isn't *really* who she *is* yet, so all's fair as long as she's ready with a backup story in case she gets caught. Anyway, Ernest accepts the misinformation without a hint of recognition. Lizzie's moral dilemma vaporizes.

Now, what is she going to feed him? He's already said he hates oysters.

On the way home, Lizzie stops to buy a bottle of California Cognac for herself, and a bottle of the French stuff for Susan.

Susan already has her overnight bag packed. Lizzie hands her the Armagnac. "You have been an absolute mega-sweetheart. If there is ever, ever, ever anything I can do for you . . ."

"No speeches. Let's get going. I've hidden my mail and my makeup kit. Keep the closet doors closed, and he won't notice the clothes. Now, I've unplugged the phone, so it won't ring, but we might also want to remove my number from the dial and replace it with yours. He'll recognize that, won't he? Now. You wouldn't have law books, right? Help me get them into the bathroom. We'll put them in the vanity."

"My God, Susan. You have an absolutely criminal mind."

"I've seen every episode of 'Man from U.N.C.L.E.' and all the James Bonds. I know all the tricks. I just never get to use them. It's a wonder the CIA hasn't snatched me up."

As they load the books under the sink, Susan is inspired. "If I were you, I'd put a couple of your personal gewgaws in the room."

"Right."

Lizzie selects two ragged throw pillows for the love

seat, and her silver brush, which she puts beside Susan's sink.

Susan wipes her forehead with the sleeve of her sweatshirt. Lizzie flops onto the couch.

"Can you think of anything else?"

"Well. There's the morning. You better put a change of clothes in my drawers so that it looks natural."

"Good idea. Let's head downstairs."

"I'd love to be a fly on the wall," Susan says shyly.

"If anything ever comes of this, you'll be my bridesmaid."

The sparseness of Lizzie's apartment reminds Susan of her college days. When Lizzie is gone, Susan scrunches up on the futon with Lizzie's dog-eared copy of *Bonjour Tristesse* and pours herself enough Armagnac to warm the lining of her stomach. She calls Michael to tell him she feels magical. Being part of a conspiracy suits her.

After she showers, Lizzie has time to run out and order General Cho's Chicken and Spicy Shrimp and Scallop Strategy from Hunan Delite. While she waits for the takeout, she browses in the Moon and Stars Deliteful Stationery next door. Maybe she should buy a pair of red tapered candles? Lizzie thinks Chinese by candlelight is a bit too dime-store Mata Hari. She doesn't want to give the impression of being overeager, but she has had about enough suspense. Her face is starting to break out. Something natural, fun, easygoing, and conducive to wild sexual expression? There is nothing like that in the Moon and Stars. Lizzie flips through a copy of *Cosmopolitan*.

"This is not a reading library!" says Mr. Moon or Mr. Stars.

"*Excusez-moi? Je ne parle pas Anglais.* How you say?" says Lizzie, as she continues to slowly flip through the pages. She is devouring an article entitled, "How to Handle Happiness and How to Know When Enough Is Too Much." She doesn't make it past the second page because she is utterly, suddenly, depressed.

Maybe I won't be able to handle happiness, thinks Lizzie as she rumples the sheets on Susan's bed to make them look easy to get into. Maybe I don't really want love because I need it too much, and I haven't made it as an actress because I am afraid of success, so I settle for fear of failure. Finally, she gets a grip on herself.

"I will never read a woman's magazine again," she vows.

Lizzie tests out the couch. She decides to relax. She reclines voluptuously, in the manner of Goya's Duchess of Alba, clothed version. That's all well and good for the moment, but there will be nowhere for Ernie to sit if she is lengthwise voluptuous during supper. A love seat is a love seat in name only.

Much as I have been forced to scale rocky cliffs only to discover that an alligator-filled moat stands between me and my climb up a sheer castle wall to the usual true love's turret, so is Ernest Barnes forced to brave the foyer of Blackwatch Towers. Ernest has decided to be a man about this. He is prepared to throw caution to the devil, who, I can assure you, is always ready to catch it.

Lizzie has hair the color of autumn leaves. Come what may, no barrier is greater than his desire to find out, once and for all, if she is similarly hued elsewhere. Enough with the imagination; his wrist muscles are becoming overdeveloped.

"Good evening," says Julio as he holds the door. "Haven't seen you in a while."

"Evening, Julio. I'll just go on up."

Choosing to climb eleven flights of stairs rather than risk the elevator, Ernest takes a moment to give himself a mental pat on the back. Barnes. Ernest Barnes.

Lizzie hears his shoes scrunch along the hallway carpet, stopping before her door. She waits for a knock before she leaves the love seat.

"Coming."

She counts ten Mississippis, removes a smudge of mascara under her right eye, and opens the door.

The Deed

    As Ernest passes through the preliminary portal of love, he has a sense of déjà vu. Breaking gently from Lizzie's embrace, he surveys the room. "So this is where you live."

    "Mm-hmm," she says, trying to coax him into another kiss.

    Ernest obliges distractedly. "Do these apartments come furnished?"

    Lizzie laughs and heads for the kitchen. "Well, I forgot to ask you what you wanted so I ordered my own favorites." She considers setting out Susan's dishes but they're not to her taste.

    Returning with the Hunan Delites, one plate, and one pair of hand-painted chopsticks, she cozies into the love seat.

    "I'm sure I'll like whatever you have," says Ernest, as he sits beside her, twisting away from the table to study the delicate Belgian Renaissance tapestry behind them.

    "Like it?"

    "Yeah. It's very nice."

In an attempt to ward off further inquiry, Lizzie says, "I picked it up at the Cloisters. On sale. It's one of those repros from the Middle Ages. I've kind of outgrown it though. I just haven't gotten around to getting something else."

"Really? The Cloisters?"

"You know. They've got all this stuff from all these European castles. And a very nice view. We can go there if you want."

"And I can get one of these?"

"Sure if you want. I'd give you this except I've already promised it to a friend."

Ernest shifts away from Lizzie for another look. He is absolutely certain that Susan told him that the tapestry she had, which is practically identical to the thingamajig that hangs here on Lizzie's wall, was a real Northern Renaissance treasure. Why would she say a thing like that? He is saddened that Susan would feel the need to lie to him about such a trivial thing. Why? To impress him?

Lizzie kisses his neck. "You into art?"

"Sort of." Was Susan in love with ... He removes the unfinished notion from his mind as if it were a burr.

"You know," Ernie muses, "modern furniture all looks the same to me. It even feels the same. Same squish. Know what I mean?"

"Yeah. Someday I'm going to replace this with Victorian." Lizzie pops up and paces quickly around the room scanning for telltale evidence. Excusing herself, she hurries to the bathroom and pulls open the medicine chest. She takes all the prescription bottles labeled Susan Whitbread and shoves them into a drawer. That ought to do.

"You hungry?" she hollers.

"I'm salivating over this food, if that's what you mean."

"That's not what you're supposed to say."

"It's quarter-to-ten. I'm practically dead already."

"You're supposed to say, 'Only for you.'"

"That comes later."

Lizzie fishes a chunk of Spicy Shrimp and Scallops out of the cardboard box and pops it into Ernest's mouth. "Good, huh?"

"Not as good as you," says Ernie.

"Ooh. Well done! Young man, you have a future."

What Lizzie does next is even spicier than Hunan Delite's tender delicacies. Taking the matter into her own hands, she caresses it until Ernest feels faint.

"Oh, God," says Lizzie, as she extricates herself.

"What? What?"

Lizzie covers with a passionate kiss. "I've got to, uh, you know."

"Yes, yes. Whatever."

He closes his eyes and thinks sexy thoughts to keep himself hard. He assumes that the slam he hears is the slam of the bathroom door.

No time to wait for the elevator. Lizzie pounds downstairs to her apartment. "Susan! It's me. Oh, shit. Oh, shit."

Susan wordlessly attempts to struggle to a standing position from the depths of the folded futon as she watches Lizzie rummage through her worldly goods for her diaphragm. She finds it. It is dusty from disuse. She grabs her Ortho-Gynol and dives out the door. "I am such an idiot!"

Lizzie bolts into Ernest's arms. "Sorry. Woman problems." Ernest is in a fuzzy erotic heaven and needs no explanation. He barely finds the strength to pull off Lizzie's blue jeans before he releases his desire inside her. There is no time to research her pubic coloring until his breathing once again becomes regular.

Having satisfied his curiosity, and his pent-up passion, Ernest satisfies the more than willing Lizzie, but not, I feel it is important to add, as thoroughly or as deeply as

Prince Charming would have done. There are awkward moments. Fingers lovingly moved from the right spot to the wrong spot; frenzy when slow motion would have been the proper speed, and vice versa; Lizzie's attempts to telepathically implant knowledge of her nerve endings indicate to her that Ernest, for all his good qualities, is not psychic, and she is too shy, this being their first time, to make her requests aloud. Even so, because she is now completely convinced that Ernest is me, she is thoroughly content with second best. Lizzie runs her fingers along the inside of Ernie's thighs. Ernest twiddles Lizzie's nipples, as he readjusts to find a comfortable way to sit on Susan's love seat.

Ernest is thinking that if he ends up sleeping on the love seat, he will have back pain for a week.

Lizzie is making crucial decisions. She will go to the bank tomorrow, take the savings with which she was planning to run off to Greece and meet an Anthony Quinn look-alike, and invest in a roomy convertible couch so that she can entertain in her own place. She will tell Ernie the truth—eventually. She will exercise regularly from now on. She will give all the clothes she doesn't wear to the Salvation Army. She will read the newspaper every day so that she will always have something to talk about. She will do this and she will do that. She will not, however, advise Ernest of her ambitions or her impending thirtieth birthday. Experience has taught her that Mother was right. "Wait for the rock," then dole out the hard stuff.

The morning after their night of love, Lizzie awakens in Susan's bed. As she listens to Ernest breathe, she yearns for a jar of Ben-Gay. The back of her legs and the inside of her thighs remind her that she's out of the habit of love. She crawls quietly from under Susan's down comforter and creeps into the bathroom. After soaking her thighs into submission and schpritzing herself with a bit of Susan's toilet water, she sneaks between the sheets. Ernest wakes from a dream about forgetting to file his income tax. He is glad to be awakened, but the remaining vestiges of his dream and his urgent need to get out of Blackwatch before he's spotted interfere with his ardor. As he dresses, Lizzie pulls the comforter over her head and wonders why he's in such a hurry.

"I'll leave with you," she says, knowing it is far, far worse to lie alone and mull over what might have gone wrong than to get to work before the coffee shop is ready with the day's first pot of brew.

Julio Puts
Two and Two
Together

Julio the doorman is no spring Chicano. Last night he thought that Marcy's man, Ernest Barnes, looked too hunched over to be doing right by his main woman. He walked too fast for a man who hadn't been coming around for some time. Something had happened. Marcy didn't seem lonely, but she might be. Too much coming and going. Julio kept his daughters at home as much as he could, so that his wife could watch them without troubling the Virgin Mary, who must already have her hands full watching over the women in Blackwatch Towers.

Marcy is too thin. Julio wants to tell her that a husband likes a bit of flesh to hold on to. Instead, Julio tells her to carry an umbrella when he hears rain on the forecast. Marcy needs a man to take care of her. This Ernest Barnes, he didn't take care of Marcy so much. He let her stay too thin. He left her alone. He maybe wasn't such a nice guy and wouldn't marry her.

When Ernest Barnes came one day to see Susan Whitbread, Julio didn't know what to think. First of all, Susan Whitbread almost never looks like a woman. Wearing suits all the time when God gave her a shape to be proud of. Walking fast fast fast in flat shoes. Julio knows what Susan needs, but he doesn't think Ernest should give it to her and Marcy at the same time. Susan needs a real man who will make her know she is a woman; Julio doesn't picture Ernest as the one for the job. Maybe this Ernest did give it to her anyway because in the past few days she looks like her muscles are not so tight around her mouth and her hips sway.

And now. Now he knows that Ernest Barnes is a danger man, a bloody-fanged wolf.

Julio sees Ernest Barnes walking out of the building not with Miss Lightner and not with Miss Whitbread but with that *guapa* one, Lizzie Edmunds, whose hair is colored like a mango fruit. Now Ernest Barnes averts his eyes from Julio, which proves that he is guilty.

"Be careful, miss," he tells the innocent victim.

Lizzie says, "Morning, Julio." Julio scowls at Ernest.

Holy Mother mark his words, any daughter of Julio is not living alone without a father or mother or a husband to see that she does not find out what men are like.

When he sees Marcy, he is sad for her. "Miss Lightner, how are you today? You look tired. Is everything feeling okay these days?"

Marcy says, "Oh, I'm tired, but I'm real good, really."

Julio is moved. "I always know you are a very strong woman. Don't you worry."

Marcy nods indulgently and scuttles over to the library to research theme parties which have oblessed the noblige throughout history.

Stress

Ernest doesn't give a hang about doing work for W, P & H this morning. What the hell, he thinks, I'm a partner. I don't have to work anymore. I'm in love. Who can I call? Ernest picks up the phone and dials his mother in Wisconsin. They chat for a while, but he doesn't mention having found the girl he wants to marry, because he hasn't yet mentioned breaking up with Marcy. Mom is fond of Marcy. When they met, Marcy showed a real interest in her apple brown betty recipe. Ernest stays in his office with his door closed because he is certain that if he goes anywhere near Lizzie his feelings will be obvious to anyone who sees them together.

By noon, he is feeling claustrophobic.

Hearing Susan and Lizzie share a laugh, Ernest emerges from seclusion.

"What's funny?" he wants to know.

"Nothing," says beautiful wonderful glowing Lizzie. Ernest silently prays that she has not spilled the beans.

"That's good," he says. Susan is holding a very un-Susan-like satchel. "What's that?"

"It's a gym bag. I'm going to the gym," answers Susan, who doesn't want to get into a discussion about it.

"Why?" asks Ernest.

"Why do you play racquetball?"

"For business reasons."

Lizzie gives her sweetums a strange look.

"Well, I am going to the gym for abdominal reasons."

Ernest assumes she means she has some woman problem and asks no further questions. "Sorry."

Susan emits an amused "tsss." Lizzie shoves her fist in her mouth to block her laughter. Ernest becomes uncomfortable. He thinks they know something he doesn't. Maybe he should not have kept the door closed all morning.

Taking Susan by her elbow, he leads her out the office door. "I'll be back in a moment, Miss Edmunds. Take messages, please," he says as if everything is normal.

"Certainly, Ernest. May I call you Ernest?" giggles Lizzie.

"All right, which one of you guys had a three-martini breakfast," mutters Susan as she glances back at the tittering temp. "Was there something you wanted to discuss?" Susan asks as she finds herself face to face with Ernest in the elevator.

"What's going on?"

"Nothing."

"Were you and Lizzie discussing anything?"

"Nope. Just having a good time."

Ernest wants to ask what kind of a good time. He wants to be in on the fun, to know everything about anything about Lizzie. He wisely restrains himself. "She's a nice girl, isn't she?"

"Very nice. Too bright for the job, really."

Ernest doesn't answer. Susan is wondering why Ernest shepherded her into the elevator. He seems to be staring at her. She has never felt unsure of herself alone in an elevator with Ernest. Now she does. She doesn't know why. She watches the numbers light up as the elevator heads to the lobby.

"I want to tell you something," he says finally.

"Okay," says Susan.

"I am in love. I thought I ought to tell you. You being responsible, you know, for setting me straight."

"Well, I thought something was bothering you." She can't leave it at that. "With whom?"

"A woman."

"I appreciate your openness," she says, surprised at the irritability in her own voice.

"That night we went to the Stanhope. That turned everything around. I've done some serious thinking since then."

Susan runs her tongue over her bottom lip. It is sharp and chapped. She doesn't want to hear what Ernest might say next.

Ernest kisses Susan's cheek. "Thanks."

When the elevator reaches the lobby, Ernest doesn't step out. He holds the door open.

"I just wanted you to know."

She has an urge to flaunt. She doesn't quite know where flauntage ends and unprofessionalism begins, but that doesn't hold her back. Swinging her gym bag over her shoulder, she says, "I just want you to know that I, too, am in love."

"That's really...goddamned...beautiful," splutters Ernest.

He's actually really goddamned annoyed. He feels an unusual pinch in his lower intestines and lets go of the door. By the time the elevator reaches the fifth floor, he is in a four-dimensional rage. Susan belongs to him. She's his partner. She has become utterly unreliable. Christ. Ernest draws a stream of air through his teeth. There's nothing wrong, he tells himself. It's caffeine. He entertains brief second thoughts about Lizzie. She drinks caffeine. So did Marcy. This morning, he had a cup of coffee just to be polite but if the relationship was going to work out they were going to have to have a confab about that.

Susan doesn't witness the actual effect she's had on Ernest, but she feels happily wicked as she whirls an extra time through the revolving doors. She considers the possibility that she might have lied to Ernest when she said she was in love. What does she know? She has very limited expertise. Her research has been equally limited, and until recently, out of date. It may very well be that she is in love, but she doesn't think she has defined to her own satisfaction what love is, so she is reluctant to form a conclusion. It was still fun to toss that little grenade at old Ern.

When he returns to the office, Ernest hazards a kiss. Lizzie senses he's in a snit, but says nothing. She has a thing or two of her own to chew on.

While Ernest was downstairs, Lizzie checked her answering machine. There was a message from the woman who handles all Canardino's casting, Ann Hedonia. Lizzie prays that Hedonia doesn't really remember her or her tongue. Maybe then, she'll have a chance.

"You look happy," grumbles Ernest.

"I am happy. Aren't you?" Lizzie hasn't known Ernest long enough to find his moodiness anything but kind of cute. He reminds her of her grumpy grandpa. "Give me another kiss."

Ernest isn't prepared to risk exposure. "Once is lucky, twice is tempting the fates. What if Honoroff walks in?"

Lizzie doesn't argue, though she rightly suspects that if Honoroff walked in and saw Ernest Barnes fondling the temporary secretary, Ernie would probably earn himself a warm spot in the big man's heart, not to mention an invite for drinks at the Boys Will Be Boys Club.

Ernest is behind closed doors when Lizzie leaves at

one. It's just as well. She's so nervous. She has a callback in Hedonia's office. Canardino will be there. She is, at this very instant, making rash promises to God about what she will do if she gets even a teensy-weensy part in a Canardino picture.

Marcy rests her head on the table as she waits for the next packet of nineteenth-century society columns under the peeling frescoes in the reading room of the Public Library. Suddenly the design and execution of a party for the purpose of ingratiating Ellis Yuppington and his assistant, Magenta Smarm, to a troupe of socially influential aristocrats who have, for whatever reason, failed to garner plummier invitations seems meaningless. She can't concentrate.

Poor Marcy can count the times David Hightest has declared his love on one finger. And that finger was used on the first night they were together. Since then, he has remained mum and cagey, as Marcy's occasional—though not nearly as much as she would if she felt she could lavish freely and be lavished upon in return—declarations fall splat on the floor and David answers in silence or a noncommittal hug. It's hard not to take this personally.

Furthermore, unless her bathroom scale is broken, she seems to have gained another three pounds despite an ongoing case of Aphrodite's revenge. A current total of eight pounds has been donated to her thighs in the name of misbegotten love.

Marcy is wearing the same jeans she's worn for the past four days. That's all she can manage. She wonders how great lovers in days of yore kept their figures and got their laundry done. They didn't. Most of history's great love affairs were conducted by members of the ample-bodied leisure classes, which is to say that somebody else did the catering while Juliet and her boyfriend pined. Rarely was Prince Charming involved, and as a result most of these relationships didn't work out. Somebody ended up dying instead of living happily ever after—except in the case of Wallis Simpson and the ex-king, which I personally supervised as a favor to a very dear friend.

With a glance toward the ravaged ceiling she wonders, if she were to get collagen injections for younger-looking skin, would things be different?

When Marcy was hired to cater the party for the opening of the Total Perfection Spa, she received partial payment in the form of a membership valid until she loses her looks or the year 2000, whichever is sooner. It would do Marcy nothing but good to head over there and allow herself to be ogled by the aspiring male actors who hang out at the juice bar. Marcy doesn't feel up to donning her high-cut Spandex leotards and musk perfume.

She needs the safe comfort of gray sweats and no makeup. She decides to work out far from the manly crowd until she can't stand the way she smells. She heads for the YWCA, where, as lucky coincidence would have it, she nearly stumbles over Susan, who is struggling to achieve her eighteenth sit-up while retaining her dignity.

"Where the hell have you been?" she pants as her shoulder blades hit the mat. "I've been trying to reach you."

"What are you doing here?" Marcy has never thought of Susan as the fitness type.

"Well, if you returned my calls, you'd know. Nineteen...twenty...Now let me die in peace."

"I'm sorry," says Marcy. "I've just been a bit... preoccupied."

Chewing the Fat

Marcy sucks up Susan's description of what she calls her "situation" with unusual interest. For one thing, it is entirely unexpected. For another, it gets her mind off her own problems with Hightest.

Marcy says, "Yeah. So it's like you don't know whether you actually love him, or maybe he stands for something—like something you don't have in yourself, so you love him sort of symbolically—or whether you love him because he's the first guy in ages who doesn't have some kind of a complex."

"I don't know whether he has a complex or not. Maybe I don't know him well enough."

"Yeah. That's like David. I mean, this guy gets along with my clitoris like they're old basketball buddies, but mindwise, we don't totally connect. No doubt he's very smart—I mean, after all, he's a shrink—but he doesn't want to talk about things with me. I can't even get him to give me the definitive answer on whether or not he's married. He considers that an outside issue. You'd think someone in the business of listening would be delighted to talk for a change. Maybe if I charged him by the hour, he'd be more comfortable."

"Michael talks to me, but not professionally. He's a mime, for chrissake. Definitely Type B. Possibly C. I don't mean to sound prejudiced, but is that a way for a grown man to make a living? I can't imagine him escorting me to a cocktail party, or fitting in when the conversation turns to creative finance. But I like him. A lot. Maybe he appeals to my recessive rebel genes. I don't know. That's the problem."

Marcy suggests that they jog around the indoor track. Susan doesn't jog. It jars her breasts. So they retreat to the sauna. Susan leans on one hand and holds her towel closed with the other. Marcy lies flat on the boards, unconcerned with modesty.

"I don't know either," says Marcy. "I'm sort of yin about it most of the time. Although something has happened to make me feel a bit yangish, which kind of knocks me out of balance. Not that I'm not yang some of the time. It's just the distribution is different since David."

Susan doesn't answer because she cannot remember whether it is the yin or the yang that stands for the feminine half of existence so she is hard-pressed to understand what it is Marcy thinks David is doing to her.

"All I can figure," Marcy sighs, "is that She neglects him. She probably makes him feel inadequate or something, so he comes to me, and I give him the love he lacks with her. I mean, if he were satisfied, would he be running around?"

"Maybe?"

"No. She doesn't treat him right. The bitch."

"She's probably not so much of a bitch. She's probably a woman just like you who's stuck with a guy who can't make up his mind."

"You're so cynical. Whose side are you on? How's Ern? Is he coping?"

Susan dispenses with modesty as the hot air of the sauna becomes difficult to breathe. She lies down on the bench below Marcy.

"I should say so! He's madly in love quote unquote."

"Oh, Jesus."

"You're not still in love with him?"

"Get out of here. Is she famous? Is she beautiful? No, I don't want to know. Don't tell me anything. What's her name?"

"He won't say."

"He's on the rebound. She's taking advantage of his weakened emotional state. What would any cookie worth her chips want with a man like Ernie?" Marcy hovers close to tears.

"What did you want with a man like Ernie?"

"He has no business getting over me this quickly! What was I? This cheapens our whole relationship."

Susan pats Marcy's sweaty back as Marcy weeps over her replaceability.

"Marce, what did you think would happen? I mean, how did you think things would be when you grew up? Anything like this?"

"Not exactly," Marcy answers, as she wipes her face. "I had planned to marry Paul McCartney, but he threw me over before we even met. Then there was Prince Charles. But I couldn't stay a virgin forever, so I wasn't even in the running. I liked James Bond, but he was a womanizer and he traveled a lot, so at some point I went for Ernie."

"I would have gone for guys like Ernie, but they didn't seem to go for me. We have too much in common, I guess. To tell the truth, Marcy, I grew up to be the man I thought I'd marry. I know what I expected: doctor, law-yer..."

"Indian chief?"

"Not unless he was also an MBA. I'm conventional. I'm supposed to have money, respectability, a VCR, a food processor, all the right things. I'm supposed to live in the right places. I've got that. So what do I get from a man besides sex?"

"Other things."

"Yeah, but I don't know what I want so how do I know when I have it?"

"Don't ask me. You want to meet an MBA? I know one."

Susan has a silent crisis of conscience. Should she want to meet someone else if she is weighing the possibility of being in love with Michael? Maybe the thought that she does is all the proof she needs that it isn't love at all.

"Okay," she says sadly.

As they dress, Susan and Marcy agree that Susan will casually drop by fifteen minutes after Ellis's scheduled arrival time. Then Susan will spontaneously come along with them to the Post-Nuclear Bar.

"I can have an idea about his party or something," says Susan.

"Susan, if you do have an idea then you're way the hell ahead of me and I beseech you to tell it to me. I get paid buckets to be a slicing dicing idea-o-matic and I haven't a molecule of inspiration."

"What about the Constitution?"

Marcy cannot hide her disappointment. "Oh. Everyone's sick of the Constitution. It's been done to death."

"Well." Susan has never been tired of the Constitution and she hopes she never will be. "What about a fresh approach?"

Out of desperation, Marcy forces herself to consider the idea.

Susan leaves the sauna. Moments later Marcy joins her in the crowded shower room.

"I love you!" Marcy hollers as she heads for the shower next to her friend.

The room empties quickly, leaving the two women alone.

Susan decides she will never return to this gym. Marcy ignores the attention. "You are an absolute talent, Suze. We'll take the Constitution concept, see, and play with the language in a culinary way."

Susan turns off the shower and steps away from her friend. "I don't know. I think those women thought that when you said you loved me you meant like, love."

"Listen. The Eurotrash will love it. I love it. It's American. It's chic, and we can get away from California cuisine! You're a brilliant puppy."

Susan towels her hair. She thinks that she needs a good cry to clean out her confusion. But Susan is not a crier. She tries to will her eyes to water, but they don't.

"Will I like this guy?" she asks Marcy.

Practically Suspending
Disbelief

Lizzie walked to Hedonia's office so that she could prepare. As a result of the dry spell after her Froot Loop Toucan days, her confidence had rotted inside her until she was hollow. Now she had a matter of minutes in which to putty up the hole. I'm beautiful. I'm talented. I'm ready. If the director wants me to sleep with him I probably will. No, I won't. Not unless I like him as a person and it is the starring role and Ernest could never find out. But then I will have to lie to Ernie and I couldn't do that so I'll have to give up either Ernie or my career, and I can't do either. Shit.

Lizzie stops at a newsstand and purchases a packet of Reese's Pieces. If it worked for E.T. maybe it will work for her. At the very least it ought to prevent her stomach from roaring in the silence of Hedonia's cold appraisal.

The Filipino houseboy matches the double oak doors of Ann Hedonia's upper East Side town house down to the lemon-shined brass. This, Lizzie muses, is class. Act natural.

"Upstairs. First left," says the houseboy.

"Oh, thank you very much. First left. Right up the stairs. Okey doke." My God, now you've blown it. No movie star babbles to the houseboy. They'll know you're a fake. Shutten zie up, she scolds herself, savagely biting her lip in self-punishment.

She draws air through her mouth and exhales through her nose. Straightening her back, she enters the room. She smiles what she hopes is a restrained but pleasing smile, but she is concentrating so hard on controlling herself that her eyes don't focus properly on the people in the room. "Good afternoon," she says wondering if she should have said a more casual "hi" or introduced herself.

She hears three hellos. Recognizes two. Comforted by the familiarity, she ventures a look. She remembers Hedonia, a dark-rooted L'Oreal blonde with Clairol highlights and a formerly pert pink-rimmed nose that has sniffed the high life. She is chubbier than Lizzie recalls. Turning her voluptuousness into a great advantage, she wears a tight cashmere sweater and a dusky blue suede skirt.

Canardino's quack is unmistakable. This is the voice, until now all but faceless, that prompted her first and only rebellion against the horrors of auditioning. Had she known how handsome he was she might not have stuck out her tongue.

He is everything that is alluring about the Italian male. Easy sensuality, shining black hair the color of squid ink pasta, full lips of a beet pasta pink hooded by a slight stubble, and those weighted eyelids shielding eyes of fresh spinach pasta green. Lizzie loves to eat pasta. Should it become necessary, doing likewise with Canardino will be eminently tolerable as long as she has earplugs. His voice is a jealous angel's revenge. Unforgettable.

Lizzie finds a seat. She's relaxed now. She doesn't care because she knows she doesn't stand a chance.

There is only one other person in the room. Lizzie has never heard her voice, but she knows not only the face, but almost every square inch of flesh on this famous *Sports Illustrated* swimsuit model. Kasha Varnishka. The milky-skinned Yugoslavian beauty.

"Miss Edmunds, I'm Ann Hedonia. I'm sure that Mr. Canardino needs no introduction. And this is Kasha. Lizzie Edmunds."

Lizzie nods.

"Some time ago," begins Chuck Canardino, "you auditioned for one of my films. About a middle-aged computer executive who mortgages his home to purchase silicone breast implants for his mistress who is carrying his surrogate child. I didn't cast you."

Lizzie nods and smiles.

"... But I didn't forget you. Not since third grade had anyone stuck such a striking tongue out at me. Spirit. That shows spirit, I thought to myself. Maybe we are looking at the next female Dustbin Holstein here. But you also have looks. A red, pointy tongue. Talent. And more than enough *je ne sais quoi*. So I thought we might be able to work together."

"Thank you," says Lizzie. "I'd like that very much. Um, would you like me to read?"

"Let me tell you a little about the project. Kasha and I have been looking for a vehicle—"

Kasha spirals out of her chair and begins to pace. "Aye em seek of the sweemsuits. I study philosophy in Jugoslavia and I weesh to mek a feelm wheech expresses pairhaps what an Jugoslav vooman must go through to succeed in the capitalist vorold."

Chuck takes a moment to admire Kasha's gleaming Eastern Bloc teeth. "I came across a script that I thought had some promise. It was about an émigré who becomes a doctor by being a daytime hooker and going to night school, but her hooking is discovered by the dean of the medical school who falls in love with her. He wants her to humiliate him, but she wants to bury her past. She ends up treating venereal diseases of teenage boys and initiating them into the ways of safe sex."

Lizzie gathers that she is not competing with Kasha for the title role. She further gathers that she might actually already have a part and she is, deep down, a smidge disappointed that she will not have to compromise herself with Canardino. "Mmm. Sounds good."

"It is one of the highest concepts I've ever come across. So I had it rewritten by Morton Hand. He added his homey masterful touch to the human side of things. Then Joe Filet rewrote it, adding his own accessible but perverse humor. I then had Queen go over it to improve the suspense quotient so that Bill Silverstein could polish the dialogue to a crackle. Then Kasha . . ."

Kasha smiles and her nipples spring to erection beneath her silk blouse.

"Kasha suggested that it was lacking the women's touch. So we gave the hooker doctor a best friend. That would be you."

Lizzie feels dizzy. Is this ecstasy? Canardino smiles at her.

"It would be an honor to work with you and Kasha," says Lizzie.

"Yais," says Kasha. "We awl vork in sairvice to such a screept."

"Every *mot* is a *bon mot*," adds Canardino.

"Ent we haffent even finished."

"What's the best friend like?" asks Lizzie.

"Warm. Wonderful. Spielbergian. Spunky," says Chuck. "We're still developing the part. Mandi Seidelchester is working specifically on her role. We may add an extraterrestrial element. But I'm not sure. I don't go for gimmicks."

"It would be the opportunity of a lifetime," says Lizzie. "Incidentally, I can also roll my tongue."

"Hexalaint," Kasha agrees. "Do you mind shawing your braists?"

"Now?" asks Lizzie. She wonders why she wore yesterday's graying white cotton bra again today. Was it a subconscious self-destructive impulse that will undo her at the last moment?

"No. Een preencipal."

"No. In principal. No. Not at all. If it serves the story," says Lizzie, who can only begin to conceive of the embarrassment of seeing her slightly floppy bosoms each four feet across on the big screen, much less how her family would feel. They're my tits, she decides, and I'll do what I want with them. "Nothing exploitative, I hope. That is, unless exploitation would sort of serve the story."

"Not to worry," Chuck adds. "The star will have most of the gratuitous breast imagery. You'll just provide backup."

"That sounds fine," says Lizzie. "You don't want me to read?"

"Actors don't need to read. They don't even need to act," says Canardino. "They just have to be."

"What a beautiful man," says Ann Hedonia. "You are lucky to cut your teeth with Canardino, Miss Edmunds." She raises her clipboard, turning to face Lizzie more squarely. "You are a member of SAG?"

Miss Hedonia is not referring to the self-help group formed to help actresses with mammary droopage, but to the Screen Actors Guild.

"Yes," says Lizzie. "I did a commercial a while back."

The rest of the conversation involves financial arrangements. Lizzie does not get a good deal. She barely gets a wage. But she gets a chance, and Hedonia knows a chance is worth more to an actress than money to buy food, which, ultimately, only makes a girl fat and unsuitable for most parts.

Lizzie leaves with the peculiar feeling that she has just gotten a part in a movie. A major part. But she's not sure. She didn't read or show them a résumé. They never said, "You have the part, Lizzie Edmunds." But they talked money. And it seemed that she had the part. But she doesn't want to assume.

With primary casting out of the way, Hedonia, Canardino, and Kasha Varnishka plunge into a production meeting. The first order of business: food. Ann Hedonia has a friend of a friend who heard Max Shotz swears by this woman named Marcy Lightner. "She's a honey of a caterer. Hot. Very Hot," she says.

"No donuts," says Canardino. "I cannot have donuts on the breakfast wagon."

"Lord no."

"Vaht does she look like?" asks Kasha.

"She's, you know, catereresque. I don't know if she does movies, really. I know she did the Total Perfection Spa."

"Shuck, I must have thees."

"I don't know, honey."

"Shuck, why is good for Total Pairfection is not good for Kasha? Perhaps you tink I am eenadequated?"

"Get Lightner."

Lizzie looks at herself as she passes by a window. Her hair has a gold-dust sparkle. She notices people noticing her. They are looking at a star, not a temp. She is the real Lizzie now. She doesn't want to dilute the strange, almost complete happiness which has infused her body. W, P & H is nowhere to go on the most glorious day she has had in all but thirty years. She decides instead to take the afternoon off to go to Macy's and actually order the couch she's promised herself so that Ernie can come over to her real place and make real love with the real her for real.

Lizzie stops into a pharmacy, walks right up to the counter, and unashamedly purchases a box of multicolored condoms and has them gift wrapped. She's always wanted to do that. She's not sure whether to give them to Ernie for a giggle or mail them to Ellis Yuppington anonymously and hope that they arrive at an awkward time.

After fifteen minutes, she finds a working phone booth that is not adjacent to a construction site. "Hello? Susan?" she croaks into the phone as if the greeting took all her energy.

"You sound terrible."

"I had Thai curry for lunch and I think I should go home to rest. The coconut milk."

"By all means. We'll see you tomorrow," says Susan kindly.

"Tell Ernest, will you?" Lizzie says.

When Susan gets off the phone she tells Ernest that Lizzie ate Thai curry so she'll be home sick for the rest of the day.

Ernest doesn't believe a word of it. He dials her at home. It is as he suspects. The machine greets him warmly. He attempts levity. "I hear you're not long for this world. Would you be free for dinner before taking your last gasp? Don't call me here. I'll get back to you in an hour."

Ernest calls in an hour, an hour and a half, and two hours. By four o'clock he is (A) on the brink of panic, and (B) certain that Lizzie will slip through his fingers and into the arms of another man if he does not act decisively. He learned his lesson with Marcy. He hates the thought of coping with two once-in-a-lifetime loves lost. There hasn't been a deep-breathing exercise invented that will rid him of that kind of stress.

At four o'clock he leaves another message on her machine. "If you are not having an affair with another man, will you mar...uh, move in with me? I love you and I want to have a viable relationship."

Severing the connection with his finger, he allows the receiver to remain nestled between his shoulder and his chin as he tries to determine whether he has been emotionally decisive or merely rash.

An Unscheduled Appearance

Marcy left the gym feeling that she had performed a mitzvah, an undeniable karmic plus. That helped. Life is not altogether knotted and gnarly if one can do good for one's fellow woman. With watering eyes, Marcy entertains the idea of becoming a sort of Mother Teresa for the unattached.

It was, Marcy surmised, totally preposterous that Susan Whitbread was having an affair with any man, much less one who wore makeup and leotards. But was she one to judge? Marcy has been forced to broaden her definition of preposterousness to avoid falling into it.

You may be wondering: What became of the whirling bachelorette who was ready to sparkle love dust on a newer, more exciting lover every week until she decided which man would be hers? Well, what indeed. She miscalculated. She misunderstood herself. These things happen.

Despite her gift for self-deception, on nights when she can't sleep for wondering whether David is making love to the Other Other, Marcy is willing to admit that almost more than she really wants David, she wants to win.

David's four o'clock patient has canceled because she is flying to Martinique and has to pack. David has conceded the power of Marcy's allure by squeezing in a four o'clock assignation *before* the 5:30 cocktail party being given by his Other Other.

The prickly twinge Marcy feels is not altogether unpleasant. Since there's a bit of time to kill, she decides to wander the city streets, savoring her wonderfully tragic romantic twinge, alone amidst the unfeeling throng.

Doubtless, you have observed that Marcy is not especially alone. Your own love life sometimes seems to have been singled out to endure complications unimaginable in your mother's day. Aphrodite blames this on me. About fifteen years ago, I briefly suffered from colitis. I do not mind the occasional gash from a sword swipe picked up in pursuit or defense of my beloved, but colitis was humiliating. Illness forced me into a partial slowdown, some results of which are regrettably still with us. There was some discussion among the higher-ups regarding my ability to withstand the pressures of the job. After centuries of achievement! Legends! Lifetimes of happiness for countless damsels! A certain dour saint, who shall remain nameless in the spirit of good taste, proposed that there was no reason at all why damsels should look for paradise on earth if it was to come to them in heaven, and that my job should be eliminated entirely. She was shouted down by the others. Aphrodite, whom you know I usually adore, suggested the creation of other Prince Charmings, and the possibility of forming a sort of Academy Charmant, to be run by her. Her position was that there weren't enough to go around. She presented a portfolio of boys, all handsome and on the brink of puberty, she thought might be recruited to learn the arts I so lovingly practice. I kept my calm, letting others argue the merits of her idea. Everyone knew she had ulterior motives. She was dying to get to Paris and ply her charms by employing the one-stop shopping concept, gathering the finest young male flesh in the world at one convenient location. She is not as energetic as she once was. God listened politely, but he does what he wants. He determined, citing recent cost-benefit analyses, that to increase the quantity of Prince Charmings from among the ranks of *Homo erection* would be to greatly risk sacrificing the quality I have strived for and, in all modesty, achieved. I thought that was the end of it, but I have just learned that Aphrodite is on the campaign trail again. Perhaps you think she has a point?

No matter what Aphrodite thinks, my long-gone colitis is not responsible for *all* the romantic confusion in the world.

At this very moment, Marcy *thinks* she wishes that someone would come along and solve all her problems by sweeping her off her feet. Seeing a lone tear trickle down her comely cheek, I am inspired.

I materialize as the Tall Dark Dashing Stranger of her dreams, complete with the hairy forearms she secretly finds attractive. I station myself at a hot dog stand down the block. Suddenly Marcy feels a craving for an all-beef frank with mustard and onions.

"No sauerkraut," she says without looking me in the eye. As she rummages for a dollar with which to pay me, I work my magic. Marcy feels heat rising through her body. She grasps the handle of the hot dog cart to steady herself against the intensity of her instant passion.

Electricity surges from my hand to the dog to her delicate fingers as I hand her her frank.

"My heavens!" sighs Marcy, as she struggles not to

drop it. "I mean, thanks." Shuddering with spontaneous orgasm, she staggers to a nearby bench and devours her hot dog. When at last her nerves cease vibrating and her muscles regain their normal tension, she wonders how a hot dog man could possibly affect her, a four-star caterer, in this way. "May I have another one?" she sweetly inquires.

"As many as your heart desires," quoth I.

Marcy eyes my forearms with undisguised lust. "Who *are* you?"

"Marcy, I am not really a hot dog vendor, but Prince Charming. I have materialized to sweep you off your feet and make all your dreams come true."

She laughs! Awe silences me. Fair Marcy laughs and shakes her head! "Serves me right," she says as she walks away without taking her second frank.

As she rounds the corner, the clock strikes four. Marcy remembers with a familiar prickle that she and David have a scheduled tryst between four and five. At the same time she realizes that the hot dog vendor called her by name.

"I'm late!" Marcy cries as she involuntarily raises her arm to hail a cab. It comes too soon. The meter is ticking. She hesitates. The cabbie leans on the horn. He's in no mood. Marcy jumps in the backseat and the cab is rolling before the door shuts.

"Go around the block. Drop me at the hot dog stand."

"Whattahellzamatterwitchew, lady?"

"Shit," she says with the voice of one condemned. "All right. Okay. Take me to Blackwatch Towers."

Moments later the cab stalls in traffic. Marcy weeps, fearing that she may never see me again.

"Listen, lady," growls the cabbie, "it's not my fault. There's a parade down Fifth Avenue."

* * *

Marcy dashes past Julio without a greeting. She annoys the other tenants as she jingles her keys in the elevator. Nothing matters except getting to David. She needs him now. Now that she has hurried away from the Tall Dark Dashing Stranger, leaving him behind forever, she needs the reassurance of David's strong arms, his kisses. She needs to hear him tell her, once and for all, "I love you. I want to be with you. I will leave her tomorrow, no, tonight, and whisk you away from all this to Papeete for an all-expenses-paid vacation."

But David isn't there.

Marcy is left alone with herself. She numbly pops a bag of popcorn into the microwave. She takes off her clothes, letting them fall on the kitchen floor, as she stares into the open refrigerator. The beep of the microwave timer causes her to jump. She removes a stick of butter from its wrapping and puts it in a pot to melt.

By 4:28, she feels, if not better, at least philosophical. Until she hears the sound of keys in her front door lock.

"Hi!" calls David Hightest without a trace of remorse in his voice. "There was a parade on Fifth Avenue, and one of the Mets was signing autographs!" It is then that he sees Marcy sitting cross-legged with an empty glass bowl in her lap. She is naked, greasy fingered. Her face is blotchy from crying.

"Where were you?"

"You're upset," he observes. "Were you worried?"

"No." Marcy licks the butter off the fingers of her left hand before pushing a lock of hair from her eyes. "I was furious. Now I don't care."

David says nothing as he seats himself beside her. He wishes he'd stayed to watch the parade.

"Do you love me?" Marcy asks.

David puts an arm around her shoulder and sighs. "You know how I feel. Why do I have to say it?"

"Because."

"I don't want to deal with insecurity in my off-hours."

To her own surprise, Marcy finds herself screaming, "Is that what I am? Is that what I am, your *off*-hours? And what is *She?* Your *on*-hours? I need more than this, David!"

David feels a familiar chill working its way up the inside of his body. "You sound like my first wife."

Marcy is silent in the face of the ultimate reprimand. David senses an advantage and kisses Marcy's buttered breasts.

"I want to talk," she says. "I want to know about you. About what's going on."

"What do *you* think is going on?"

"Don't give me that psychiatrist stuff."

"I sense some kind of feminist hostility toward male power figures. Isn't that a little out of date?"

Marcy is stung. She *hates* to be accused of being out of date. Setting the empty bowl next to David, she walks to the kitchen sink. She wets a paper towel and wipes the butter and popcorn dust from her body. She picks up the clothes from the kitchen floor and dresses.

"I was a bit upset. Sometimes I wish you could spend more time with me. A whole night, maybe."

"I think She suspects."

"Maybe She's seeing someone herself!" Marcy retorts.

"She wouldn't do a thing like that," says David in her defense.

"C'mon, David. How important am I to you? Am I ... I mean, if I want more, am I wasting my time?"

"You know my situation." David feels overwhelmingly tired. He looks at his watch.

Marcy returns to the couch because she is afraid that if she stays in the kitchen she will take a knife from the top right-hand drawer and commit homicide. David takes her hand. Marcy doesn't resist.

"If I said that it was either me or her, what would you do?"

"Be sad. You can't have everything."

"But *you* can. I mean, if I were to walk out right now you wouldn't bar the door and beg me to stay."

"It's your apartment."

"But I mean you wouldn't fight to keep me?"

"Do I look like one of the three musketeers? Look, I value our time together. But you're free to do whatever you need to do," says David.

Marcy feels so constricted she can barely breathe. She opens a window and leans out.

Ellis arrives promptly at five. In his opinion, being late is decidedly downscale, and he makes a point of allowing plenty of time to get to his destination. Not long ago *W*, the fashion tabloid for semi-garmentos and the chicgnoscenti, reported that promptness was IN, and although Ellis would claim not to take such an edict seriously, as taking *W*'s IN and OUT list seriously would be exceedingly OUT, it does have a subtle but distinct effect.

Julio rings up, forcing Marcy to draw her head inside the room. David reclines on the couch with his eyes closed.

"Send him up, Julio," says Marcy. David doesn't budge.

Marcy examines her face in the mirror. Not bad, considering. She splashes her eyes with cold water. She doesn't have time to do even a quick version of her beauty routine so she smears some Natural cover-up over and under her lids and pinches her cheeks for pink. Returning to the room she says, "I have a client coming."

David labors to his feet. "I'm sorry our hour is up. Maybe we can reschedule later in the week. Believe me, I know that women face a great deal of stress as a result of the man shortage. And I'm sympathetic to that. But frankly, Marcy, I thought you were different."

Marcy regrets not killing him while she had the chance. Saying nothing, she opens the apartment door and waits for Ellis to reach her welcome mat, which he does. She kisses him on the cheek, something she has never done before, and waves him in. "Ellis Yuppington, I'd like you to meet Dr. David Hightest."

David scratches his ear as he waits for Ellis to decide how to handle the situation. Ellis offers a wet iceberg-lettuce handshake. "A pleasure to meet you," he says.

"Mmm," says David, as he power-grips Ellis's hand and looks him psychiatrically in the eye. Ellis looks away. He's not paying for this, so he doesn't have to put up with it. But he doesn't look away for long. He's already dreading the discussion at his next session and he doesn't want to provide David with more material. He notices that David's socks appear to be cashmere. David notices Ellis looking at his feet, and slips them into his unscuffed Gucci loafers. I bet I keep him in shoes, thinks Ellis, shoes that *W* has clearly deemed absolutely OUT for at least two years.

"Well, Marcy, Mr. Yuppington, it's been a pleasure. Unfortunately I have a five-thirty engagement," David effervesces, while showing himself to the door. Marcy doesn't follow him out. Ellis is too busy wondering what Hightest is doing here to mind his manners. David waits a moment for response. Getting none, he shuts the door behind him.

Marcy collapses on the couch.

"Are you all right?" Ellis asks her. "Shall I make you a cup of tea?"

"You're sweet. No, thanks. It's just..." Marcy sits up and expels a lungful of air. "You ought to be inoculated before you go near a person like that."

"What do you mean?" Ellis asks, without disguising the desperation in his voice.

"He's untrustworthy. He's evasive. Just generally speaking, he's a disease."

"Oh." Ellis feels queasy, but he can't immediately access the meaning of his feelings so he doesn't know whether he is traumatized or suffering from the side effects of a feta cheese and sun-dried tomato pizza. "May I use your bathroom?"

Susan Prepares to Meet Her Destiny

Susan leaves work early and has a manicure. She then escorts her coral nails home, where she spends most of the next hour dressing for her spontaneous introduction to Ellis Yuppington. She decides on the sexy pink sweater and a straight wool crepe skirt. With twenty minutes to kill before her estimated time of arrival, Susan shuffles papers. She tries to work, but can't concentrate well enough to remember what she's read.

The phone rings. "Hello beautiful one!" says Michael. "Guess what?"

"What, handsome face?" says Susan, hoping she betrays none of the discomfort she feels.

"I don't know whether to tell you now or in person. Are you coming over later?"

Susan hesitates.

"Shall I tempt you?" Michael teases.

"You already tempt me," says Susan honestly. "It's just . . . I'm drowning in work," she lies. "But how about, say, ten?"

"Perfect."

"But tell me the news."

"Step into my parlor said the spider to the fly."

"Seriously."

"Later, love buckets."

"Love buckets?"

Michael blows several kisses into the phone and hangs up.

Susan checks herself in the mirror. She is prettier after talking to Michael. She wants to call him back and say she'll be at his place, in his muscled arms, as quick as the Metropolitan Transit Authority can carry her, but she doesn't want to do it enough to actually do it. Besides, she doesn't see how she can cancel her carefully unplanned rendezvous when Marcy will be waiting for her. Bad manners are not her style.

Too Much for One Day

Lizzie is carrying so many packages that she has had to splurge on a cab. The cabdriver helps her carry her bags to the lobby of Blackwatch Towers. Julio leaves his post to help her haul her maroon Macy's bags to her apartment.

"Is your birthday?" asks Julio.

"Nope. I think I got a part in a movie, Julio. I'm celebrating."

"You need a bodyguard?"

Lizzie giggles. "Not yet. Can I make you a cup of coffee?"

Julio has to get back to the lobby.

Lizzie takes a seat on top of one of her red bags. There are six altogether. She figures that if she didn't really get the part and she is suffering from delusions and has imagined the whole thing, she will be consoled by this shopping spree until her insanity is discovered and they put her away somewhere. No, she tells herself sternly, temporary insanity won't get her off the hook. With Amex debt as her constant companion, Lizzie has no choice but to make a complete commitment to personal success. Either that, or perish in a blaze of bad credit.

The message light on her answering machine is flashing. She doesn't want to play back her messages. What if she's sane and she did get the part and there's been a mistake and they've taken the part away from her?

She's not ready. Ignoring the flashing message light, Lizzie picks up the phone and dials information.

"The number for Thomas Morrissey, please."

"Business or residence?" asks the operator.

Lizzie's latent movie star hauteur raises its high hand. "Business, my dear. Thomas Morrissey is the hairstylist who got Jackie Onassis to abandon Kenneth!"

The unimpressed operator connects her to the talking computer.

Ashamed, Lizzie reprimands herself for getting hoity-toity with information. When the computer finishes repeating the number, she says, "Thank you."

Morrissey is closed. Her purchases are unbagged.

There is nothing standing between Lizzie and the beacon of doom. Bravely, she presses the replay button.

She hears Ernie's dinner invitation, three hang-ups, and this: "It's me. If you are not having an affair with another man, will you mar . . . uh, move in with me? I love you and I want to have a viable relationship."

She plays the message again, meticulously parsing each sentence. So. He was going to propose but he backed down. Why? Does it mean he wants his milk without buying the cow? What does he mean by love? What does he mean by viable? If he didn't suspect her of running around would he be asking this? And finally, why does he have to bring this up on the day she has gotten her first major part and invested all the money she has, and then some, in redecorating her apartment?

If Lizzie was dealing with Prince Charming, she would not ask herself these questions. She would be sure, surer·than she's ever been about anything in her life. She lies down on her futon in corpse pose for five minutes, during which she loosens all her muscles and thinks of nothing, nothing, nothing, except how to get Ernest to go the whole nine yards, what to do if he does, how her decisions will affect the prospects of meeting me or Paul Newman, and what all of the above will do to affect the delivery of her new green velvet couch.

Realizing that relaxation is for others, not for her, Lizzie dials. "Ern?"

"Oh, hi," he says cautiously.

"I got your message."

"Oh. What do you think?"

"I just got in."

"Where were you?" he asks, hoping to sound casual.

"Wait till I tell you about my day."

"I can't. I'll be right over."

Why all of a sudden does he want to come over? Lizzie feels a trace of annoyance. "No. I'll come to you."

"Bring a suitcase. I might not let you leave."

"Oh, yeah?"

All the Way

Lizzie stops at Les Fleurs to create a bouquet of red carnations, roses, penis flowers—the Latin name of these shiny broad-leafed beauties with the long, hard stamens slips her mind—and assorted autumn leaves.

"Are these for me?" Ernest is staggered. What a gal. In all his years of flower giving, he's never gotten a bunch in return. "You are absolutely the utmost!"

Lizzie removes her coat to display the next wonder, her brand-new body-hugging green suede suit. Ernest's admiration is mixed with worry. He knows he's looking at at least a thousand dollars' worth of dead livestock. This is not the garb of a temp. "You win the lottery, Lizzie?"

"Sort of," says she as she pulls her auburn hair off her neck, piling it on top of her head and then letting it fall.

Lizzie's clothing, the flowers, her sensual pose, please Ernest, yes. But he begins to sweat. Something out of his control is going on, and he doesn't know what it is.

He mixes himself a soda water with ice. "Anything to drink, sweetie?"

"I don't know. Yes. Do you have vodka?"

He opens the freezer and pulls out the remains of a bottle of Stolichnaya. He brushes away the frost. "With?"

"I don't know. Maybe straight."

Ernest pours a cautious thimbleful into a glass.

As if by an unspoken contract, the drinks are taken, sip by sip, in silence. "Now what?" says Ernie.

Lizzie shrugs. She's not ready to divulge her magnificent secret. She's still not dead sure someone won't take it away. Ernie wants to talk about his B-level proposal, but he wants a clue to Lizzie's reaction before he brings it up.

No one's talking. There is only one thing to do and they do it. Ernest fiddles with Lizzie's green suede jacket as if the buttons were covered with grease. She wriggles out of her skirt. He lowers his pants to his knees, and away they go, until they mildly and mutually explode. Nervous tension evaporates. The natural remedy has been proven to be more effective than either Advil or Tylenol.

"Why don't we go out to eat," says Ernest as he runs his hand up and down the slight tummy bulge Lizzie intends to lose.

"I'm so happy with you," Lizzie answers.

Ernest pulls his pants up and zips the zipper. He can't stand the suspense any longer. "Lizzie..."

"Ernie, I notice you always put your pants on before your shirt and then you unzip your pants to tuck in your shirt. How come you don't just do your shirt first?"

"Where do you go at lunch? Where were you today? Where are you when you aren't with me? I need to know."

Lizzie fastens her bra. "Well, Ern. I wasn't going to tell you quite yet."

Ernest buttons his shirt, unzips his pants, tucks in his shirt, and rezips his trousers. "You're right. We're both individuals. You can have your own life."

"Why, thank you very much," drawls Lizzie.

Ernest paces as if to dodge the blow he's expecting.

"Ern, I've been auditioning for parts. I'm an actress. I just got a part in a Canardino film. Today!" Lizzie grabs Ernest in midpace and holds him still. "Not the lead, but next best next to Kasha Varnishka."

"A Canardino film! You mean I just did it with a movie star?" Ernest kisses his movie star girlfriend with more passion than he showed his temp girlfriend, but something causes him to pull back. "You weren't acting before, were you?"

"Were you?"

"Why didn't you tell me?"

Lizzie shrugs.

"I want you to live with me."

"I can't. I just ordered a new couch and I'm redecorating my apartment."

"I love you." He gazes into her eyes.

"I love you, too." The gaze factor doubles.

"What if I ask you to marry me?"

"Does that mean you want to make a commitment?" Lizzie steps back to scrutinize her lover. Then she smiles in a way I have waited for her to smile at me. Oh, that lucky, unworthy lawyer.

"Let's just say I could use a new couch," says the knave who has stolen my Lizzie's heart.

I am ill. I have had a very difficult day. Despite the odds, I had hoped for better. Dearest Lizzie tests the limits of my patience. As always, I understand. I know she's turning thirty; I understand with intolerable clarity why she's pledging her troth to this Barnes, but I find it unbearable to contemplate. I lose often, I confess, but not well. I hardly thought it possible, but now *you* are even more precious to me than before.

Appropriateness
at First Sight

For me, turquoise is neither soothing nor a particularly pleasing shade of blue, but it is, for reasons obscure, the predominant color of the Post-Nuclear Bar. Turquoise and a burnt brown. The sky and the charred remains. The symbolism is not lost on me. It is merely fatiguing. I am hardly in the mood.

I am too exhausted to disappear, so I duck into the bomb shelter room to get myself a drink. Because it is not time for any of the women crouched over their postapocalyptic cocktails, I disguise myself in a modacrylic lime green sports coat. With my thumbs pulling my belt loops, I adopt a cocky swagger. I splash my neck with English Leather and don secret agent sunglasses, which make it difficult to navigate this dark and rubble-strewn room.

I order a gimlet from a squat and muscled young woman named Patsy. Patsy doesn't believe in me anyway. She pushes her helmet away from her eyes and says, "Vodka or gin?"

I sit well away from the table Marcy and Susan share with Ellis Yuppington as I sip my gimlet from a Philippe Starck "can de tin."

They're laughing. I'm glad to see that. Ellis loves Marcy's concept. He agrees that a Constitutional Send-off Gala will attract the titled nobility and the attention of *Vanity Fair*. He is no less impressed with Susan, who, at least physically, meets almost all the requirements Ellis has outlined as necessary for *the* woman in his life.

"Nice Rolex, Susan," he says.

"Thanks, Ellis."

"When Rolexes were eclipsed by Tiffany's new line, I almost caved in. Then I decided the heck with that. It's a good watch and I see no reason not to stick with it."

"I'm not too trendy, myself," Susan admits.

Marcy deems this an appropriate moment to excuse herself. "I'm going to the little survivors' room."

I nod at her as she passes, but she doesn't notice. She looks straight ahead.

Now that they are alone together, Ellis seizes the opportunity for an intimate chat. "You athletic?"

"I do a little this and that. Swimming, when I can," says Susan half-truthfully.

"Tennis?"

"Not really."

This is a minor strike against Susan. Ellis has always fantasized about a woman who can beat him on the courts. "Too bad. Swimming's a total exercise though. A mind-body thing."

"And very refreshing after a day at the firm."

"I'm entrepreneurial," Ellis confides. "Perhaps we can find a way to interface."

"That would be nice."

"I really like the cut of your jib, Susan."

"I like your jib, too."

"Want to continue the evening later? A movie?"

"I'm busy later," says Susan.

Ellis is roused by this smidge of resistance. "Then tomorrow."

Susan is torn. This Ellis is the most appropriate man she has ever met. He's clearly a fast-tracker. And he's interested in her. How things have changed since she took up with Michael! Susan feels so lucky, she's afraid to test her luck, or lose it by testing too much. But she'll probably do it anyway.

"I have an opening tomorrow, but sometime later in the week?"

"An opening?"

"My boss and his wife invited me. The Prado sent over a massive exhibit of Northern Renaissance art, which is my first love. I can't miss it."

As he presses his business card into her hand, Ellis feels the stirrings of a high degree of compatibility. Susan is a ballpark approximation of the square hole his round peg has been fantasizing about—and more than he dared expect in one package. Hell, he thinks to himself in the heat of infatuation, so what if she's not a blonde?

Post-Post-Nuclear Test

Michael has prepared a late-night supper of Cornish hens stuffed with miniature apples and doused in tarragon cream sauce. He has carved a heart in the back skin of Susan's hen, a golden brown tattoo. When he presents the bird, her eyes water. She stands and puts her arms around him, holding him very tightly. He strokes her hair.

"Only you would think of something like this," she says, knowing that there are no other words for the tenderness she feels, and the confusion.

Michael laughs. "That may be true."

It's a quiet dinner. They watch each other, link legs under the table. Michael brings out a crème brûlée. "Made it myself."

Crème brûlée is Susan's all-time favorite calorie bomb. "This is some feast."

"I...There's a festival of mime in Arles. They've asked me to perform, and teach."

Susan has never considered the possibility that mime is something grown-up people would have a festival about. She has never considered that there might be a mime besides Marcel Marceau who could perform, much less teach, in France. "That must be quite an honor. You must be very good."

"Don't you know that?"

"I should," says Susan seriously. "I guess I haven't thought about it that way."

"I've been pro for almost ten years."

"That's when I started law school."

"I want you to come. Three weeks in France. Wouldn't that be the best? I know Provence. There's a two-star hotel in the Vaucluse where they catch trout out of the stream and cook it up for dinner right in front of you."

"Beautiful. When?"

"Well. It's short notice, I'm sorry to say. Some screwup on their part. Uh, next week. Please, please come."

"Next week?" Susan's eyes water for a new reason.

"I know it's sudden, but you're a partner. Can't you do what you want?" Michael takes her hands. "I want you there."

With her finger, Susan scrapes the last of her crème brûlée out of the bowl. She thinks about the differences between Michael and herself. They are so different. Too different. "Oh, jeez, Michael. I can't just pick up and go for three weeks. I wish I could. I would give anything to be there."

"Not anything." Michael twists one arm around the other. He reconsiders. "I'm sorry. That's not fair."

"We're really kind of different."

"Yup," says he. "That's usually good."

"Yup," says she, but she's not sure.

"What about a week?"

"We'll see. It'll be hard."

"We'll just have to make a lot of love before I go. Store it up."

191

"That, I can do," says Susan. "Oh, Michael... I don't know...."

She orders herself not to think. They leave the dishes on the table. There will be time later. They tumble hard, kissing, rubbing against each other to force a fusion that will take away all the differences between them.

The next morning, before she leaves for work, Susan throws up. She thinks that it must have been the cream sauce mixing with her post-nuclear cocktail, but that's only because she's never been pregnant before.

Michael insists that she rest. The flu is always going around. He makes her a cup of chamomile tea and a slice of toast. She lets him tend to her. He smooths the blanket over her the way her mother used to do in the days before Susan distrusted leisure and love.

Weighing In

After slicing six bananas into the batch of banana nut bread dough Marcy is preparing for one of a certain well-known socialite's famous home-cooked breakfasts, Marcy takes a taste. It's good, but needs nutmeg. She takes a tablespoonful. Now it's superb and, as she admires the next spoonful and the next, she consumes the batter. All of it.

She hasn't the ingredients to mix a new batch, so she slips a coat over her splattered sweat suit. A walk to the greengrocer will burn off some of those calories, she tells herself, knowing that she'd have to shovel two tons of coal and speedwalk to Cleveland to counteract the effects of her batter binge.

As soon as Marcy finishes baking the second loaf, and the well-known socialite's indecently handsome uniformed chauffeur/lover picks up the bread, the tea, the ready-to-cook omelet mixture, the strawberries, and the crème fraîche, Marcy turns to the eight-inch pile of bills she has been neglecting.

"I've gained eleven pounds and lost a lover," says she

as she separates the envelopes into categories. Phone. Electric. Elizabeth Arden. The four *B*s: Bendel's, Bergdorf's, Bonwit's, and Bloomie's. Fred the Furrier. Fred the Courier. There are eight red envelopes she doesn't recognize. They can't be valentines; wrong season. Maybe they're love letters from a secret admirer. No return address.

She opens the first. It's from Love at First Sight.

> *Dear Fellow Love Seeker,*
>
> *Our records show that you have an outstanding Love at First Sight video. In order to ensure maximum romantic success, it is important to keep available men in circulation. If you wish to date video #11238, please notify us. If not, please return the tape so that other scintillating single people can find deep personal fulfillment.*

The remaining seven letters are, in chronological order, increasingly insistent. The last accuses Marcy of being a log on the road to love and insists that Love at First Sight will take immediate action if she does not return *Dick Judd* to their shelves.

So consumed was she with pursuit of the unattainable David Hightest that Marcy had forgotten about *Dick Judd*. She doesn't even know where she put the tape. Then she remembers. On the day she met David she bought an ostrich-skin drawstring tote. She had been using the pony skin up till then. She runs to the closet. There is a plastic bag at the bottom of her pony-skin satchel. In it is Video #11238.

She is about to phone Love at First Sight to explain that she is finished with men and will henceforth seek satisfaction on a solitary basis when she has a second thought. Marcy hesitates in front of the VCR, weighing the cassette in her hand. Not yet.

She takes a bubble bath. Puts on her white satin robe.

Schpritzes herself with Amour Fou. Feeling like she is inhabiting a Claudette Colbert movie, in fact, feeling as though she might redo her entire apartment in white quilted satin, she dusts off the Lalique goblet Aunt Lillian gave her for her thirty-first birthday—Lillian promised to present Marcy with the other five on her wedding day—and pours herself a Diet Coke.

Now.

Susan Endures
the Happiness
of Others

Have you ever noticed, my darlings, how when a great deal is happening at once, change after intense change in a small space of time, time itself seems to move differently? For Marcy, time scrapes along like a little boy heading home to get a spanking. Every hour is long. Halfway through, she is waiting for the next hour so that night will come and she can go to sleep. For Susan and Lizzie, there is dizzying vividness to every minute, and each minute seems as rich as an hour. Eternity packs easily into a week, with plenty of time left over for washing lingerie in the sink.

Sometimes Lizzie feels as though she's living in her own best fantasy, she tells Susan as she picks the raisins out of a pumpernickel roll.

When Lizzie announced that she would be leaving Witkin, Pritkin & Harris to co-star in a Major Motion Picture and marry Ernest Barnes, Susan thought Lizzie deserved a suitable send-off and *she* deserved a suitable explanation. Susan is beginning to think of her office as a bubbling tarpit of lust.

"It's a wonder my hair didn't completely frizz out with all that steamy stuff going on under my blind nose."

Lizzie smiled. "We were pretty discreet, huh? But even Ernie didn't know I was an actress. I'd gotten to the point where I didn't want to aspire in public, if you know what I mean."

Susan looks around for a waiter. "I'm really happy for you."

"Thanks. You know, this is the first time I've been in the Russian Tea Room."

"I thought it was show-bizzy, for a special occasion. I haven't been since I was a little girl. My grandfather used to take me after the ballet."

"Is it the same?"

"I don't know. I only remember the tablecloths and the pastry cart."

Lizzie watches Susan roll blinis and then copies her technique.

Susan rescues a glop of sour cream and caviar which has fallen back onto her plate. "Ernie seems happy."

"Yeah."

"Are you?"

"Yeah. He says I make him feel like a real man. That I'm everything in just the right proportions. And he's the same, mostly. He's so stable. And he's very smart. He considers all the angles. But I'm not used to things working out. To tell you the truth, I can't quite relax. The more certain he seems, the scarier it gets. I'm practically moved in, but I'm still thinking maybe I should keep my own lease and sublet for the first two years. They say that if something's a disaster, it usually falls apart by then."

"You don't sound very optimistic."

"These days you've got to be a blazing optimist to even begin to brave the odds against. But we're totally in love. It's not him, of course...."

"Well, I'm sure you'll live happily ever after," says

Susan, as her eyes water and she wonders what deep inner deficiency makes love considerably less simple for her than it seems to be for everybody else. "Want some dessert?"

Lizzie indulges as Susan looks on. The sight of cake makes her queasy. She excuses herself and sits in the powder room until she feels almost normal. Then she slips Ellis's card out of her wallet and makes a quick telephone call. She's been Ellis's utterly chaste dinner companion twice this week. Suddenly she feels more than the urge to merge. She feels compelled to exercise her deferred option to leverage a friendly, but total takeover.

"Wonderful," she says, when the baffled but not green male in question unquestioningly accepts her turnaround, "eight is fine."

She returns to the table without a word about either her decision to conduct a quasi-adulterous love life or her grinding stomach.

"You look flushed," says Lizzie.

"Reflected glory. We'll miss you round the office."

"You have to come to my premiere. Besides, Ernie considers you his absolute best pal, next to me. I'm sure we'll see a lot of you."

Being Ernest's best pal other than Lizzie, Susan is treated to the ravings of a man in love with someone other than her not long after she returns to work.

Ernie steps into her office and closes the door, though there is no longer anyone sitting at the secretary's desk. "So? What'd she say?"

"The usual. How wonderful you are and all that."

"I can't tell you how lucky I feel."

Susan smiles with relief.

Ernest, however, finds it within himself to let loose a torrent of emotion that would crack the Hoover Dam. "Susan, it's, it's, frankly, Susan, it's profound. She makes me feel like a real man, a provider. And she's a real woman. So delicate. She's always asking my advice about stuff. She's so impulsive. It's different than Marcy. I feel needed for something more than just...whatever it was Marcy needed me for. And loved. It's really the best. And, not that it matters, but I've seen pictures of Lizzie's mother so I know she'll age gracefully. She's practically thirty now. I couldn't believe it when she told me. How old does she look to you? I took her out to Lutèce. Do you think that was the right place? She seemed crazy about it. But you wouldn't think she was pushing thirty, would you? And never been to Lutèce. She has this sweet naïveté, don't you think? And on top of that I certainly hadn't counted on being married to an actress. Between you and me, I figured that she was more the tax deduction type, but her talents just add to her charm. She's amazing really. Maybe she'll be famous. I'll be turning Robin Leach away from our door. I heartily recommend this love business to you, Susan, on a serious basis." He hesitates. Susan thinks that he is through, but he isn't. "I want you to be my best man."

"The best man is usually a man."

"Don't be so bound by convention. Loosen up. You'll be my best woman, for chrissake."

Susan smiles, and restrains herself from saying that they're too far down the road for that.

"I'm very happy for you," she says.

Later that night, Susan fucks Ellis's brains out on behalf of Ernest, and Michael, who telephoned to say he'd be delayed a week because of an offer to appear on French television. "That's wonderful. I'm very happy for you," she had said. "I'll miss you."

Ellis considers this sexual bonanza a sublime experience second only to the time his stock in Digital Equipment rose twenty-five points in one week and, without benefit of inside information, he sold before it went down the next day.

He's a little taken aback by Susan's capacity for passion. Does his appropriate dreamboat have whorish tendencies which would render her more fun but less appropriate in the Mrs. category? Ah, well. He'll discuss it with Dr. Hightest at their next session.

As he plays with her hair, Ellis murmurs, "I bet you'd be really gorgeous with blonde highlights."

"So would you," Susan retorts.

Ellis finds himself possessed of a pounding erection. Nothing arouses that man like insouciance.

The Theory
of Evolution

When dealing with the manly persuasion, 99.97 percent of the time if you change the rules, the whole game changes. This *was* in the bible but it was edited out. It used to read, "And lo, she who made him feel manly, yea, to be like unto a powerful lion of golden mane suddenly maketh him to feel threatened when she diverteth a portion of the attention with which she anointed her love like a dove anoints the chest of her beloved with pulverized worm, to another pursuit."

And so it was and so it is with Ernest and Lizzie. She, who used to be home when he was home and in the office when he was in the office, always, always ready to hear about his cases, now stays late on the shoot, and later still at rehearsal, causing him to dine alone several nights a week.

Ernest is proud of her. Ernest resents her. Ernest is confused. Ernest sulks when Lizzie comes home full of excitement for something that has nothing to do with him. She is so absorbed in her excitement she only sort of notices that her sweetums is sullen and less in the mood for a tumble than he was in her temporary days. When she does notice, she doesn't really understand. She loves him just as much. She loves him more, now that she's happy with what she's doing. "Guess what!" she chirps as she throws her coat on the couch. "I've got the forest scene! Kasha was going to do it, but then she and Chuck couldn't agree on the meaning, so she gave it to me!"

Because he's never mentioned Marcy, she doesn't tell her beloved that Marcy is catering the shoot and that she actually sat beside her during dinner break. Marcy pretended not to recognize her and vice versa. When Kasha Varnishka kindly introduced each to the other as a "grett taylent," they hugged like lost sisters.

My best performances go unheralded, thinks Lizzie.

She seats herself on Ernest's lap. Ernest cranes around the obstacle to watch a fiftyish man describe the Dodge semiannual sale while a swaying crop of dancers worship the upcoming spring line of pickup trucks.

Susan Muses

Post-coitally, Ellis and Susan marvel to themselves and to each other about how well their interests mesh, like the gears of a well-oiled Precor electronic rowing machine. She's legal. He's financial. She's a team player. He's entrepreneurial. She's orgasmic. So is he. Neither is uncomfortable with oral sex. Ellis is elated. Susan feels vaguely depressed.

Ellis walks across the room to switch on the late evening "Financial Report" while Susan stares at the ceiling. Yes, everything is a technical success. The columns add up. So what makes her resist going along with the program? Ellis ought to be the one. She could have sworn he was what she wanted, but she doesn't laugh with him the way she does with Michael. Ellis doesn't contradict her. Could she live with a man with whom she is in perfect agreement on every subject except the effect of the insider trading scandals on the likelihood of garnering a golden parachute in the event of forced takeover?

She would have thought so. Six months ago, she would have thought that any man, especially an appropriate man, would have made her life complete. Now she's fussy. And well she should be.

I have taken the liberty of invading her dreams. Lying naked between the sheets, noticing that the skin on her breasts seems slightly crepe-y despite a new fullness, Susan wonders who her Prince Charming will be if not Ellis, if not Michael.

But she censors herself! "I'm getting to the age where I can't afford to feel this way. Tomorrow, first thing, I'll go to B. Dalton and see if they have a book that takes care of this."

What will it take to persuade my dear Susan that I am coming? That all she need do is wait for me? Even now I am readying my fiery white steed—grooming his wings, feeding him fresh oats from Scotland. Will Susan settle for leather interiors and front-wheel drive when she could fly across the sky on Pegasus?

Susan closes her eyes and pretends to be asleep. Ellis returns to her side. He runs his hand between her thighs. She doesn't respond.

Ellis sets the alarm for 7:05, twenty minutes early. That way, he figures, they can schedule in sex and then grab a quick run before they get to the courts. He drifts into a dream about teaching Susan a perfect serve as Jimmy Connors looks on admiringly.

Susan waits until Ellis begins to wheeze before she opens her eyes. She's been doing a little calculating. Her breasts seem to be developing for the first time since she was thirteen. And they hurt when Ellis squeezes them, which he does, as if he's adjusting a tuner, for approximately two minutes apiece before he dives southward. The last night she and Michael were together, weren't her nipples especially sensitive? She had attributed that to basic amour and the sweet pain of parting, but in the morning she was sick. Lately she's so often beside herself that she feels like twins. Some of this she can account for.

The full moon has passed without the appearance of her period. Susan is the model of regularity. Menopause? Too young. Ellis? Too recent. Michael. That settles it. No, it doesn't. Why should it?

She laughs out loud. "Well, well, well, well, well. How about that?"

"What?" mutters her bedmate as he curls his body around hers.

"Nothing."

Babe in the Woods

The forest is more magnificent than any Lizzie has ever seen, and she considers herself quite the forest buff. Each moist leaf glistens. The slightest breeze creates elaborate patterns of light across her hands and face. Before her there are as many shades of green as there *are* shades of green. The sound of her steps is absorbed by moss.

In the heart of the forest there is a clearing. The moss is singed. Lizzie's confidence falters, but she goes on until she finds the tree so tall no one has seen the top. A bird's cry. She turns. And screams.

"Cut!" quacks Canardino. "Baby. It was good...." Canardino searches for the *bon*-est *mot* he can pull out of his repertoire.

The art director rushes into the forest with his assistants. One sprays the leaves with water from a Windex bottle while the other adds more blue to the foreground leaves because the lighting director needs to counteract the yellow light.

"Great forest," Lizzie whispers to the art director. "You make God look like an amateur."

Canardino clears his throat. "Okay, baby. Look. You're walking through the woods, right? You've just learned that your best friend has given up life as a glamorous call girl—med student and now lives in abject poverty as a divorced wife in Larchmont. Your own lover, to whom you were about to turn to help Kasha start her own safe sex clinic for teenage boys, has just confessed that he is an extraterrestrial."

"Right," Lizzie nods vigorously. "I tried to get that across."

"But I need *more*. He's just told you that he has a wife back on his home planet. That was hard enough to take but now you come face to face with his wife in her untransformed state. A blob. You are face to face with the blob that you feel stands between you and your true happiness."

"Pain," adds Kasha from the sidelines. "We have all had such experience."

"Pain. Right."

"And, baby." Chuck enters the forest and gives Lizzie a fatherly pat. "When you contort your body, turn your breasts toward camera one. All right, Lizzie? Betrayal. Obstacles. Passion. And..."

Kasha feels neglected when Chuck isn't touching some part of her body. "Chuck darleeng," she croons seductively, summoning him with an articulate glance, "may I heff a leetle word?"

They confer. The crew waits.

"Okay. We're going to break for an hour. Lizzie, keep that energy up."

This lust break is unscheduled, so Marcy isn't there to feed the masses. Lizzie retreats to the production office so that her mood will not be broken by conversation. She intends to meditate, but the phone looms, begging for her to use it.

"Ern?"

"You finished? Maybe we can get dinner."

"I wish I could, but I'm squaring off with a blob after Canardino finishes poking Kasha."

"A girl's gotta make a living," snarls her sweetums. He's been reading up on this Canardino. Ernest cannot see himself telling Honoroff that his wife does pictures for that sex-obsessed sleazemonger. He knows damned well Honoroff would run out and grab a gape at Lizzie's scantily clad body, magnified across the screen for the legal community to leer at. "Why can't you do Ibsen for chrissake?"

"Listen, Ern. I'm on the verge..." Lizzie senses she's heading for a collision and changes tracks at full speed. A deep breath. "I'll make it up to you later. I love you," she singsongs.

Ernest doesn't notice or appreciate Lizzie's masterly diplomacy. Jane Pauley would never abandon him this way. And anyway, she does news. Her blouses are buttoned up to her neck when she's on camera. She'd do a husband proud, and still have time for supper, twins, and the twice-weekly-at-bedtime connubial cuddle. Furthermore, Jane Pauley would never say anybody was *poking* anybody.

"All I have to say, quite frankly, is that we're experiencing a real quality-time deficit, but at this point, quite frankly, I'd settle for some quantity time. When, by some coincidence, we happen not to be otherwise engaged, and in the same place at approximately the same time, and we happen to find ourselves together, quite frankly, I'm giving odds that we'll be too damned exhausted to make up anything but a list for the Chinese takeout. If that."

"Not now, Ern. We'll deal with this later, okay? I'm trying to keep my energy up."

"That's my point exactly."

Dinner for 1.5

Marcy has been sitting in on a personal growth course called Personal Growth Through Romantic Disaster. Miss Garwoody spends an hour twice a week trying to convince her pupils that heartbreak comes from within, and not from some lying, cheating, noncommittal weasel. "Don't invest so much," she urges, as each woman asks herself how to love without investing, and what the purpose of disinvested love would be.

"Neediness scares them away. They want you when you don't need them. Haven't you noticed?"

A fine state of affairs! I want you when you need me. I want you when you don't. I love *you*, not some idea of you. Why settle for indecisive ninnies?

All Miss Garwoody's pupils are attractive women in their thirties. They share their experiences with men. Talk about their patterns in choosing men. Talk about the misery of being with a man and the misery of being without one. About the need to compromise. And how the right men to compromise on won't compromise on them. Talk about how complete their lives are except for men.

Sometimes they go out for coffee together. Then they talk about men. Or how they ought to talk about something else.

Incidentally, Miss Garwoody has given up on H.E.'s entirely. Though she has never considered herself a lesbian, she is trying to figure out how to become more sapphically inclined in order to tap the vast underutilized love resources in the female population. Her logic is this: If women can't be with men, maybe they should be with each other. As soon as she can figure out how to work this angle, she plans to conduct a symposium at the New School: Lesbianism for Non-Lesbians.

Marcy is considerably less scarred than either Miss Garwoody or her fellow pupils. As she prepares dinner, she reminisces about her days with devoted, constant Ernest.

"Pity he was so dull," she says as she sets the table for two.

Marcy has developed a little routine that seems to take the edge off her loneliness more effectively than Harlequins.

Mealtimes, she stints on nothing. She shops carefully for a wine to complement the main course. She makes the palate-clearing pear sorbet herself.

Just before the salad course, she puts a crate on the chair across from hers. On top of the crate sits her VCR. On top of that, her television. She tastes the wine, passes judgment. And then switches on the VCR. She inserts Love at First Sight Video #11238, known to her as Dickie, and puts him on pause.

Taking her place, she presses the power button on the remote control sitting next to her teaspoon. The static clears quickly. Up comes her current, and ever available mega-male fantasy.

"Hi. My name is Dick Judd."

"Hi, how was your day?"

When she finally got around to viewing it, Marcy was so taken by the Dick Judd video that she happily paid her past-due bills and a renewal fee just so she could hang on to the tape. By now, Marcy knows #11238 by heart, so she fast-forwards to the part that she wants to see and hear.

Dick, who looks like the result of a gene splice between Redford and Newman, is standing beside his Lear Jet at the Marbella Club in the south of Spain. "...but even with all this, I'm missing something. You."

Pause, while Marcy clears her salad plate. She's having salmon steak and she has to take it off the grill. "I miss you, too."

"I'm looking for someone to share my adventures with. Someone who can surf at Eleuthera and ski at Gstaad. A woman who is not intimidated by my staggering wealth. All that money can buy, I've bought, but even with all this, I'm missing something. You."

Marcy's heard this already, but she doesn't mind hearing it again. She rewinds to the beginning as she nibbles on steamed string beans in lemon sauce.

"Hi, my name is Dick Judd. I'm thirty-six, never married, and too busy leading an exciting life to scour the planet for the dynamic woman who will be my match for life. So I'm reaching out, looking for you, my love, hoping to find you through Love at First Sight."

Marcy pours herself a brandy and settles in for the good stuff.

"Like everyone else, I like walks in the rain. The rain in my private Amazonian rain forest. Afterwards, we'll dry ourselves beside a roaring fire, making sweaty love, experiencing the full breadth of mature passion..."

The phone rings.

"Shit..." Marcy grabs the receiver. "Ernie! I was just thinking of you!"

Ernie was just thinking of Jane Pauley, but Marcy was the closest he could come on short notice. "Me, too. How *are* you?"

"Great."

Ernest hears a male voice in the background. He's already beginning to regret this phone call. "It sounds like you have company. Maybe this isn't a good time."

Marcy pushes the mute button on her remote. "No. It's just the TV."

"I'm not doing anything." Except waiting peevishly for his late fiancée to get home from the shoot. "Want to have a drink?"

Marcy watches Dick's lips move silently on the screen. She wonders about fate.

"Sure."

Maybe after all the personal growth she's been experiencing, she'd welcome a lovingly monotonous relationship with the star member of the United States Olympic Sublimation Team.

Reunion

In the candlelit darkness of the former Chez Chien Chaud—now known as House o' Weenies, thanks, in no small part, to Marcy's popular rediscovery of Coney Island cuisine—both Ernest and Marcy look better than they're feeling.

Loud music disguises the awkwardness of this reunion.

"So," says Marcy.

"How's life?"

"Still starting off with the easy questions. Well. Life is great. Business is great. Amazing. I don't even have to advertise."

"What more could a caterer ask for? Word of mouth."

Marcy laughs. "Funny, Ern."

"I do have a sense of humor, you know." Marcy used to accuse him of having lost it in the tie department at Brooks Brothers.

Marcy isn't interested in old quarrels. "I know," she says warmly. "You're looking good."

"So. You must be very busy."

"Yup."

The plunge. "Seeing anyone?"

"Mmm." Marcy's not ready to answer that question. "I heard you were fooling around with some actress."

"We're supposed to be engaged," Ernest confesses.

"I'm seeing someone too. His name is Dick." She's seeing Tom Brokaw, too. Every evening at seven.

"Marriage?"

"Maybe. I don't want to rush into anything. I've been hurt before." Marcy hopes she conveys mystery. Miss Garwoody says men are fatally attracted to mystery because they are symbolically afraid of being suffocated by their mothers' breasts and since mystery is forbidden and unmotherly, it is therefore less suffocating. Or something. Ernest suffers from asthma anyway. She wonders if a sort of primal respiratory ailment was the cause of their stunted sex life.

Ernest chews a forkful of sauerkraut as he admires the apricot-golden shine of Marcy's hair. "Your hair is so magnificent. More beautiful than I remembered."

"It's chemical. I had it cellophaned. But thanks."

Ernest tries again. "Ever miss me?"

"I'm here." Marcy swirls the chocolate around her egg cream.

"Me, too. Until very recently, I thought I'd be marrying you. I still...Everything I did while we were together is tied in with you, so when I think of then..."

"You think of me. Oh, Ern." Marcy takes his hand. Ernest doesn't allow his fingers to close around hers. Marcy hates that. He knows she hates that.

"What about Dick?"

"Don't worry about him."

Ernest isn't worried about Marcy's Dick. He's worried about his own. It doesn't belong here. He doesn't want to lose Lizzie or lie to her or go through with this.

It simply isn't nice. And Ernest is, above all else, a nice guy.

Marcy doesn't think he's being very nice to her. "Why did you ask me to meet you? I didn't come here for the chili dogs, you know."

"I'm in love."

"Thanks a lot."

"But I value your friendship."

Marcy signals the waiter for a check. "Not creativity on top of everything else. Shut up or I start swinging."

"I'm sorry," he says weakly. "But I do."

"I've got plenty of friends." She draws a deep breath. No need to be mysterious any longer. "So who is the little vixen?"

Ernest doesn't want to name names. "She's co-starring in the new Canardino film," he says, with what he hopes will pass for pride.

Marcy knows that Ernest couldn't win Kasha Varnishka's heart. He doesn't have that kind of money.

"Co-starring?" It's obvious. Lizzie. That scheming little creature pumped her for information and then stole her man. Marcy forgets that she didn't want him to begin with. She certainly didn't want anyone else to have him. She wonders how to go about obtaining a can of tuna tainted with botulism.

"She's very nice," says Ernie, "We're just going through some adjustments, I guess."

"Oh, that'll be over soon," Marcy says merrily.

"Maybe you could cater the wedding?"

Marcy shows Ernest her elbow. "You see that cut?"

Ernest examines her arm in a brotherly way.

"Would you mind rubbing some salt in it?"

Ernest pays for the chili dogs and escorts Marcy home. By the time the cab reaches Blackwatch Towers, Marcy's decided that murder is becoming an increasingly tempting solution to a number of her problems, yet she is aware that it would put her karma on the fritz for almost ever. She doesn't invite him up.

I'm grateful to Ernest, Marcy reasons. Life has new meaning. Before she loses her looks she intends to meet and marry a man so impressive that Ernest will be rendered impotent with jealousy. Lizzie will then leave him for a mega-handsome stud of bad moral character and Ernest will spend his days attracting the longing gazes of pimpled paralegals in the law library of W, P & H.

Ernest nods to Julio.

"Good evening, Marcy. Is evvating all right?"

Julio is about to go off duty, but he waits around to see whether Marcy will need him to save her virtue from this womanizing dog. She's smiling. A very bad sign.

Marcy feels shy. She's not familiar with that sensation. She defies it by kissing Ernest on the mouth. Ernest kisses her on the cheek.

"It was nice to see you again."

Julio leaves only after Ernest's cab is out of sight.

"Nice. Nice. Nice," Marcy chants to herself in the elevator. "What did you expect?"

Indeed. If all you desire is nice, go to Burger King.

When Lizzie returns home from the set, she finds her toot-toot-tootsie where she expects to find him—stationed in front of the television set.

"How's my poor, deserted darling? I kept thinking of you at home all alone and I felt so guilty."

St. Ernest, martyred Ernest, allows himself the luxury of warming slowly to Lizzie's ministrations. He doesn't plan to tell her about his evening. He's decided there's nothing to tell. And it's not lying to decide not to tell about nothing if you're not asked.

"It's all right."

"I'll make it up to you. You know, I still need you. Even if it's not the same way I used to."

He permits Lizzie to mess his head hair, but not his chest hair. He's enjoying his anger too much to give it up.

"You better," he growls. He likes the way he sounds so much he snarls it again.

Julio Deals a
Blow for Justice

1. Marcy lies to her family and spends Thanksgiving alone. She doesn't want to sit before the assembled relatives answering questions about her love life, especially when she can't provide the right answers.

2. Susan goes home to her parents. Unescorted. Mom and Dad remark on how healthy she looks and how little she eats. Susan is radiant, it's true. How a woman can have a certifiable glow and be nauseated round the clock is beyond me. I've been many things, but never pregnant.

Everything but cheeseburgers makes Susan retch. Were she in my tender care she should have cheeseburgers morning, noon, and night. Never mind that I'm not the father. I love any child of Susan's as if it were my own, especially if it is a girl.

Susan makes a point of looking everyone directly in the eyes during dinner so that she won't have to see turkey. No one ever asks Susan about her love life. Mom and Dad are secretly afraid to know, though they've never admitted it to each other. Everyone knows about her promotion to partner and Susan endures many toasts to her professional success.

Susan wears a navy blouson jacket and says nothing about the baby. She's found the best ob-gyn on the East Side. She doesn't want to know the sex, but she's listened to the baby's heart. Her baby's heart.

When Dad asks everyone to bow their heads in thanks before the meal—a ritual that has annoyed Susan since she was thirteen—Susan prays. Can't do any harm. Mom, who sits to her right, doesn't notice. She is thanking God for Susan's partnership and wondering if He couldn't manage to bestow more conventional pleasures upon her only daughter. Mom had been to the weddings of three of her friends' daughters this fall. It will only be a matter of time before the subject of grandchildren becomes as constant as the hiss in her radiator. She and Dad will move to a mausoleum in Fort Lauderdale before she'll live through that humiliation. Mom is certain that she could show her high falutin' cronies a thing or two not only about the latest in TWT—tasteful wedding technology—but about grandmothering, if God will kindly cooperate. Dear Lord, she prays, I won't make you suffer through another affair at the Maple Crest Inn. And there won't be stuffed chicken, prime rib, buttercream icing, accordions, or unasked-for advice. Amen.

3. Ernest wears a tie and charms Lizzie's grandmother.

It is Ernest who notices how, once they are away from their day-to-day lives, they feel much happier as a couple. Lizzie agrees.

Now stop your biological time clocks for a moment and ask yourself: Isn't Ernest's observation cause for alarm? Lizzie doesn't even shudder.

They rent a U-Haul to bring back the things Grandma insists Lizzie will require if she is going to hang out her shingle and become a married woman: ornate sterling silver trays that need to be polished, nine fragile crystal bowls, genuine Madeira lace tablecloths for which Grandma had never found an occasion worthy of their use, most of a Wedgwood tea service from when Grandpa had visited the Wedgwood factory, and two slip-covered wing chairs.

"For entertaining," Grandma explains. "The wife of a lawyer plays a very important function as a hostess. Doesn't she, darling?" "Darling" is what Grandma has taken to calling Ernest.

Later Grandma takes Lizzie into the bathroom and closes the door. She turns on the faucet to drown out any sound and says, "Always be a lady in the parlor and a prostitute in the bedroom."

"Whore, Grandma."

"Whatever."

Lizzie takes that as a blessing and decides it is time to clear the remaining clothes out of her old closet and give up her lease.

On the way back from Grandma's, Lizzie suggests that since they have the U-Haul, she and Ernie ought to stop at Blackwatch to pick up the last of what remains in her old place.

"Julio!" shouts Lizzie as she comes through the door. "What are you doing here?"

"Collecting triple time." Fond as he is of Lizzie, he doesn't mention the great responsibility which comes with the magnificent news imparted at his own Thanksgiving table. He is going to be a grandfather. Perhaps the greatest grandfather of all time. Angela is five months gone and swears she is a virgin. It happened once. Why not to Julio? He has led a good life. "Where you been? I thought you was in Hollywood without telling me."

"Oh, Julio."

"You don't go without giving me your autograph. Worth money someday."

"You can retire on it."

Ernest has been hovering by the mailboxes. Julio has not failed to notice the loitering Anglo dog who has burrowed himself back into Miss Lightner's life.

"Sweetheart!" Lizzie gestures for Ernest to join her. "Julio. I'd like to introduce you to my fiancé, Ernest Barnes."

Julio does not extend his hand. Poor Marcy. Poor Susing. Poor Lizzie. Each one sullied by this flimsy Don Juan. What do they see in him?

Julio knows all too well what happens when a wimming is in love. They turn so stupid. But stupid or no, they need protection. That is why Julio works out at the Fifty-fifth Street Gym on Fridays after work. Julio knows what to do in a situation. And *this* is a situation.

Julio clears his mind of all distraction. For full advantage, he places his weight on his left foot. Taking a deep breath, he readjusts his balance. A fighting machine. Ramb-Julio. He tucks his thumb into his fist, draws his arm back in an arc, and plunges his weight forward, landing a right to Ernest's jaw, pounding this man who is not a man to the floor of the Blackwatch lobby.

"I would mop the floor with you, but your hair is not suitable of being a mop!"

When Julio returns home that night he makes love to his wife so passionately that she is suspicious.

Ellis Factors
the Equation

Point one: Ellis did not get rich by dillydallying over important decisions.

Point two: All indicators seem to point to the conclusion that he is in love.

Point three: The Constitutional Send-off Gala is going to require a great deal of his time in the very near future. He'd like to have his personal dealings squared away.

Though Ellis is paying $125 for this fifty minutes, David Hightest's attention is wont to wander while Mr. Yuppington ticks off his points. After a pause, Dr. Hightest asks Ellis how he felt about their chance encounter. Ellis says it didn't bother him at all. Hightest is pleased. Together, Ellis and Dr. Hightest practice healthy self-delusion and leave it at that. Ellis wrongly assumes that his analyst and his food guru couldn't be romantically involved because Hightest isn't Jewish. Not with a name like Hightest. Marcy, in a rare moment of unprofessionalism, told Ellis that she can't stand dating Jewish men but she intends to marry one. "I don't care if he's fresh out of prison and an amputee, he's got to be Jewish."

Hightest misses Marcy's ardor. He loves having affairs with Jewish women. They're so uninhibited. But he hasn't heard from her. He doesn't feel the need to call. He's been through this sort of thing before. There are plenty of women who would be happy to climb between the sheets with *any* man, especially a handsome successful doctor. "This man shortage," he muses to himself, "gives new meaning to the concept of penis envy. I got it. You need it."

David Hightest does not experience guilt. As an American, he understands the laws of supply and demand. Did the great P. T. Barnum experience guilt while he made the most of his observation that a sucker was born every minute?

Besides, there was always Her. She'd never leave. She was a Woman Who Loved Too Much, a Smart Woman who had made a Foolish Choice, A Woman Who Loved a Man Who Hated Women. Dr. Hightest knew he hated women. That was why he'd studied psychiatry. In his youth, he'd wanted to change. Instead, he learned to accept himself.

He redirects his ear to the ramblings of his patient just as Ellis is making point seven.

"...and I feel I'm ready to make a commitment," says Ellis.

"Commitment!"

"Yes. I've decided Susan's the one. Our portfolios are compatible. Her tennis game's improving. And she's a Northern Renaissance whiz. I admit she's not quite what I envisioned in the looks department, but I've decided to compromise in that sphere. She's not bad."

"But you are making a compromise?"

Ellis falters. "Well. She's not perfect...but I'm no Greek god."

Mr. Yuppington seems to have recently developed self-esteem problems, notes Dr. Hightest. They'll have to work on that. "Have you considered that maybe you've decided to make a commitment so that you really don't have to explore your aloneness?"

"Dr. Hightest," Ellis protests, "what are you suggesting? I thought we were working towards my being able to make a commitment!"

"How do you feel about that?"

Ellis thinks he feels like Dr. Hightest's Gucci loafers are lodged in his craw, but the hour is up, so he fails to experience the feelings in his gut. He rushes home and boots up his computer.

There it is. He knows he's right, damn it. Taking all known factors into account, he's carefully graphed a compatibility curve which clearly indicates a high probability for successful merger.

He decides to go ahead with his plan. He telephones Marcy and asks her to drop off an intimate dinner for two. Marcy phones Susan.

"So. What do you want for dinner?" she teases.

"What's the occasion?" asks Susan.

"He didn't say. But there's champagne involved."

"Oh, shit," Susan titters. "I'm pregnant, you know."

"Susan! I'm in mega-fucking shock. You keeping it?"

"Of course."

"His?"

"Nope."

"Oh, shit. Poor, dear Ellis."

As she listens to Dick Judd extol the wonders of his companionship, Marcy prepares something suitable for a quick getaway—a sesame chicken salad.

One Down

Susan has been a lawyer long enough to know when she is witness to a crackerjack presentation. Ellis is doing an impressive job. She cannot bring herself to interrupt. She sits poised as a duchess on his tufted leather sofa bed. She folds her hands across her belly, though there is barely a bulge to rest them on.

Ellis points energetically to the blue and green columns on the color graph. He is blue. She is green.

At least I'm not pink, thinks Susan. "But you know, Ellis, we're very different people."

Susan knows this excuse isn't valid, but it comes in handy.

"We're both very early risers who work long days. I like to jog. You like to swim. We have a limited amount of time to spend together. No problem."

Ellis presses the next-page button on his keyboard. More blue and green. "We swim Monday and Wednesday mornings, together. And jog Tuesdays and Thursdays. Weekends"—Ellis yields a throaty chuckle; a red column appears—"I've factored in a fair percentage of *that,* too."

Susan begins to cry. Ellis smells her hair. Kisses her eyes. "Ellis . . ."

"Wait, honey. There's the matter of children. Now I know that's very important to you, and it's important to me too. We can well afford a governess, which will needless to say be a real asset when considering career continuance—unless you want to stay home, honey." Ellis unfolds Susan's hands, taking one in his own. "Personally, I'd like to hold off just a while until we've acquired a weekend place. Backyard, et cetera. I think our kids deserve the best if they're going to grow up to be hard-driving successful adults. Don't you?"

Susan is no longer trying to dry the tears that are rolling down her face. So touched is she by his architectural reasoning that she truly wishes she could say "yes." She cannot bring the word to her lips.

Ellis amends his initial scheme. "We can have 'em now if we shift some of our investments."

"Ellis . . ." Susan is in full bellow. "It's just . . . it's just so, so, appropriate. I'm sorry. Really."

Susan runs out the door. Ellis doesn't follow. He cries with only a wizened post-modern sensibility to buffer his sorrow. He's lost. He knows it. Ellis hasn't endured this kind of anguish since he was rejected from the Porcellian Club at Harvard. Don't worry about him. Never quite being able to forget the girl that he never really had, the one no other woman can ever measure up to, Ellis will muddle along until his late forties without significant pain or gain, just a growing sense of boredom, which he will inevitably attribute to the repetitious nature of the sex act or the woman he shares it with. He'll either become a Jesuit or marry a Japanese girl because somewhere he's heard they are docile, domestic sex slaves who don't mind if you take the occasional "golfing trip" to the brothels of Bangkok.

Susan lies fully clothed on her bed. Her briefcase sits unopened on the couch. She doesn't intend to touch it. She wants to do nothing. She remembers when she hated her solitude. Now, it's delicious. She knows she's not really alone, not with the baby inside her, not for at least the next eighteen years.

And Michael returns on Thursday. Thank heaven he's not coming in tomorrow. She loves him. She doesn't love Ellis. So? What's love supposed to add up to?

She has client meetings all week. It will be lovely to wade through boilerplate, drown in law, sit alone with her briefs scattered across the coffee table as she watches the evening news. Love is exhausting and you can't *solve* it. That's why she prefers litigation.

Susan remembers a promise she's made and pads down to Marcy's place.

"The chicken was delicious."

"Not too salty?"

"Perfect."

Marcy's watching *All About Eve*. Eve is scheming at full tilt. Marcy turns down the volume. "Keep me company."

"For a little while."

Marcy puts her hand on Susan's firm stomach. She presses slightly. Susan wraps her legs in an afghan. "Doesn't show yet. It's about the size of an apostrophe."

"What are you going to tell the firm?"

"That I'm having a baby and I'm going to take three months off starting July."

"What will they say?"

"Congratulations, I hope."

Marcy offers Susan a white chocolate mousse tart

garnished with raspberries and crushed pistachio nuts and takes a yogurt for herself.

"Catherine Deneuve, Jessica Lange, Ingrid Bergman, and Susan Whitbread. Next thing you know, you'll have your own brand of perfume."

One to Go

The new secretary is a man. A State graduate who took the job in order to fight reverse discrimination. He doesn't know where anything is, so Susan organizes a lunch-in-captivity for the clients and telephones the Brasserie, while Ernest dazzles Honoroff and Mr. MacLeish of the Wall Street investment conglomerate Nikoguki, Mitsuyata, Hong, Kawasan Limited with his Berlitz knowledge of Japanese.

MacLeish doesn't know a word of Japanese. He doesn't believe in it. But he is impressed by Ernie's efforts. Ernie insists that he speaks on the level of a two-year-old. Susan rejoins the meeting in time to support Honoroff's assertions that Ernest is too modest. "Much too modest."

"The Japanese respect modesty, Miss Whitbread," says MacLeish.

There's a little something the late Mr. E. B. White once wrote that comes to mind. "Soul-wise, these are trying times."

Michael was beginning to think all times were trying,

229

always. Especially in the free-lance mime biz. It was going to be nice to come home to Susan. He realized that her conventionality had a charm of its own. It revitalized him when he fought against it. When he succumbed to it, life took on the rhythm of the ocean. Nine lulling waves, and a slapper for the tenth. It was comforting to know what to expect. It was liberating to know that while he hit the high notes and bass, Susan kept perfect time. He could do without her. But why should he?

Orly was clogged, but the crossing was speeded by a sympathetic jet stream.

By 10:00 A.M., Michael was past Customs and on the phone. By 11:00, his co-conspirators—Michael has many friends and has done many favors—had gathered and been briefed.

Stomachs have been rumbling for forty-five minutes. The meeting is going well, but it's dull. Conversational gaps are plugged with ample throat clearing.

"Something's going around."

"Maybe the cook at the Brassierie caught it and died." Finally, the new secretary buzzes the conference room.

"Delivery, I think."

"Send 'em in," Susan orders.

Honoroff extends his leg, prying open the door without lifting buttock from chair.

Enter ten men in leotards and whiteface. Susan pales, but says nothing as they form a phalanx and face her. With a nod from the leader, two mimes enter wheeling what appears to be an invisible grand piano. Michael enters.

MacLeish raises his terrier brow. Susan shows no sign of recognition. Michael is unperturbed. He rolls back his invisible sleeves and passionately accompanies a silent four-part rendition of "All of Me."

MacLeish hums along. "...Why not take all of me?" It happens to be one of his favorites.

The Height of
Inappropriateness

"That," puffs Susan, as she spots the father of her child leaning against her apartment door, "was the height of inappropriateness!"

Michael ignores her wrath and adopts an instructive tone. "Hello, Michael, luminescent halogen light of my life. I've missed you desperately and craved your tender ministrations. Take me in your arms. I love you madly."

"Get serious." Susan throws herself on the couch. Michael throws himself on Susan. "Michael."

"Relax, and I'll teach you dirty French words."

"I know I've got to work on relaxing..."

"Relax on relaxing."

"...but..."

Michael lifts himself onto his elbows. "I'm sorry. I guess I'm rushing things."

Susan prepares herself to dive at the point. Confessions about Ellis are beside it. Michael nuzzles the bend of her neck.

"I'm going to have a baby."

Michael takes Susan's face in his two hands. That isn't

enough. He holds her as tightly as he can, hoping that tells her how he feels better than he can. And that isn't enough. "Amazing."

"Pretty basic, really. How was France?"

"I want to get him, or her, it might be a her, swimming really early. And make her fearless. And maybe we'll speak two languages at home so he can be bilingual from the start. What do you think? What color should we paint the baby's room? Where *is* the baby's room? We'll get a loft. Okay? And I'll build swings into the ceiling."

Susan laughs.

"I guess we should get married first."

"I love you. I just need to be sure it's real."

"What?"

"We're very different."

"That's real."

"Stop being opaque."

"You mean the love part? What's more imaginary than love?"

"Tell me about France."

Michael pulls an Hermès box out of his knapsack and hands it to Susan. She carefully pulls off the ribbon, gingerly opens the box. You don't get Hermès boxes every day. Inside is a rose-pink crocodile Grace Kelly handbag.

"It's your engagement purse."

"It, my god, Michael . . . it's the most beautiful thing I've ever seen. Did you steal it?"

"Unfurl your eyebrows and take that back."

"Sorry. This must be worth thousands!"

"Innuendo and out the other, chickadee."

"But . . . are you ever going to be able to cross the French border again?"

"Not without my wife and child," answers the sly mime grinning from cheekbone to cheekbone.

Susan weeps: one-third hormones, one-third emotional tumult, one-third grief at the thought of having to refuse this marvel of a Grace Kelly bag. "Oh, Michael. I'm not ready to get married. I have enough to deal with just being a mother."

Things Are Not
as Bad as
They Look

In an attempt to sway the already overwhelmed Susan, Michael the Mime insists that she keep the rosy pink crocodile Hermès Grace Kelly bag. "It clashes with everything in my closet," he says with a sweet modesty designed to cover up his brazen plot to convince Susan that he is all-loving and wholly understanding without being a sap—to convince her that he is *me*.

We can relax. Susan is overwhelmed but she is not unhappy. Susan is plain and simple adjusting to just how happiness feels. And that'll do it to you.

She made partner. A life's dream. First woman in the firm, to boot. She made a baby. No more mooning at the Alice in Wonderland statue. And Michael ought to keep her comfy cozy until I come along.

Six months ago Susan wondered if she'd wandered into a late-model Embittered Career Girl Movie. No more singing along with "Who Put the Men in Menopause" for her. She'll have her happy ending or my name's not Prince Charming, or Charmant as they say in France, or Fronce, as they say in Grace Kelly movies.

If Susan keeps her troth pledging at bay—and I have faith that she will not buckle, having come this far—Michael will probably resort to flinging accusations that she is an FOI victim in her face. He will produce a persuasive list of symptoms. But Susan does not suffer from Fear Of Intimacy. She suffers from faith, as many faithful have.

She will wait—with the purposeful serenity of a single mother who has a challenging profession and can afford an English nanny—for the perfect degree of appropriateness and *total* happiness that I embody.

Sneak Preview

Ernie zips his fly, puts on his shirt, ties his tie, unzips his fly, and tucks in his shirt, just as he always does. Only it's his best suit, his best shirt, and his most powerful power tie. Lizzie insists that he take it all off and wear his Girbaud dessicated jeans and his preweathered leather jacket.

"The shirt's okay." Lizzie slides into her black leather pants.

Ernest has never been to a screening before. "Lillibet." Ernest has taken to calling Lizzie "Lillibet" because that's what the Royal family calls the Queen. "I've been watching 'Enviable Glitz Tonight' for four years, and everybody is always dressed up for a screening."

"That's a premiere. Tonight you are going to sit in a little room with squishy seats and screen what they hope adds up to a movie. And don't clap when it's over unless everyone else does."

"But I'm proud of you."

Lizzie wriggles into a low-cut black silk blouse. She removes the leather pants and dons a black linen skirt.

Too late in the year for linen. The green suede. But not with a black blouse. Too frowsy. The green suede, the hot pink turtleneck casually bunched up around the waist, and Jesus H. Christ, why does she only have black flats? It'll have to be black tights and the V-neck green sweater. She pulls it low so her lacy black camisole will show. Kasha may have two little fig breasts to die for, but she hasn't got cleavage. Lizzie has cleavage. Voluptuousness is in: Check your *Vogue*.

Tactful Ernest knows better than to comment. He has seen enough movies to know that actresses are nervous before their audiences. Then they shine. Ernest is looking forward to seeing Lillibet shine. She's been a bit testy lately.

She'd say the same about him, but just when she's ready to pitch it, he turns adorable and she's happy again. When she's happy, she's so pretty that Ernest gets happy, too. Until one of them gets cross.

That, as Mia Farrow's old childhood hubby used to say, is life. Mia divorced him and went on to better things.

There are no klieg lights. The screening room is located on the tenth floor of a scrungy Broadway building. Ernest can tell the Money People from the talent. Money People take one look at this place and refuse to check their coats. Canardino oozes and kisses and pushes Kasha Varnishka forward to shake hands. She is nervous. Ever mindful of the dangers of being seen in real life, Kasha strains to keep her back to the direct light. This evening she noticed little laugh lines that no amount of NeoVisage Enriched Molecular Formula, ten patents pending, Special Facial Line Elimination Elixir would disguise. She can't stop grinning until the lights go down. The Money Women notice lines Kasha hasn't even noticed herself, and are reassured. The Money Men think she's smiling at them, that the film business is the best business, and that they don't care if they lose every cent.

Kasha is diplomatique: "I ainvy you, Mrs. Zo-ent-zo, thet you are fascinetting to a main as hentsome as your husbint."

Never alienate the wives. This is a tenet of Kasha Varnishka's philosophy. You may one day be one yourself.

For professional reasons, Kasha makes a point of giving every Money Man present at least one dewy, wistful, lingering glance. Chuck needs additional finishing funds. Kasha wants to marry Chuck Canardino and get her green card.

I don't blame her. One thing Prince Charming cannot get a girl is a green card.

Ernest would not have minded the fine cut of *Careless Love* if Lizzie hadn't been in it. Even in the darkness, Lizzie can see the steam rising from her beloved's chair. She caresses his neck. He leans forward. All Ernest can think about is what other people are going to think when they see *his* fiancée, and altogether too much of her ample figure, on the screen. All Lizzie can think is that if Ernest can't adore her for the screen goddess she really is, well, then, to hell with him. From the sounds generated by more impartial members of the audience, Lizzie knew that when the lights went on, the Money Men would recognize her, too.

"I love you," she whispers in Ernie's ear.

Ernie nods. Lizzie knows what he's thinking. "They'll envy you, you wonk." Ernest does not want to be envied. He wants to be comfortable, which, at the moment, he is decidedly un-. The more un- he gets, the more he clams up. The more he clams up, the angrier Lizzie becomes. When the lights go up, Lizzie heads for the white wine. Glass in hand, she plays the Actress Graciously Accepting the Adulation of the Money Men. Ernie feels tired. His back aches. He wants to go home and do stretching exercises. He tenders pained smiles and overdoes the seltzer water.

"Sweetest, I'd like you to meet Mr. Chuck Canardino, my director."

Ernest shows his teeth. "Congratulations, Mr. Canardino, on the completion of your film."

"Your Lizzie is going to make the world stand up and take notice."

"That's what I'm afraid of," says Ernest who hopes the world has other things on its mind.

Canardino takes this as a joke. Lizzie doesn't. She leads him into an empty elevator and presses all the buttons.

"What's up, Ern?"

"Nothing."

"I can see that. You *could* be a little happy for me."

"I am." Ernest offers his betrothed a dry peck on the lips. "It's a little unnerving to see the woman I plan to marry melded from the waist up with some oozing terrestrial whatsis."

"Extraterrestrial."

"Well, it bothers me."

"That's my job. And I was obviously good at it."

"What does that say about your character?" The elevator stops.

"What are you implying?" Lizzie pounds the Door Close button. Ernest presses floors nine through fourteen.

"Nothing."

"Look, I love you, but this is what I do. And if you're going to take it personally, we're going to be in trouble."

"I don't know if I can deal with a woman whose goal in life is to smooch up some Martian on the goddamned silver screen. I'm not saying you shouldn't do it. I'm saying I have my limitations. And I'm wondering if you have yours."

"I'll say," says Lizzie. She pauses to fix her face in the

reflection of the stainless steel paneling. "Let me tell you, mister, you're not exactly my idea of Prince Charming."

I am delighted that Lizzie has realized this. I have been deeply concerned about her.

Ernest is silent for three floors. He is devastated by Lizzie's laser-keen perception. Finally, he speaks. "And I suppose you're some fairy-tale princess."

"Let me handle the repartee around here. Okay, Ern?" Lizzie has decided to forgive this blubbering man on the grounds that she likes a splash of jealousy. Lizzie dreads being taken for granted.

"What am I supposed to think when I, and the rest of the U.S. of A., see you making love to some Vaseline-muscled stranger?"

"One. That whoever-it-is is a homosexual. Two. That I'm thinking of you the whole time."

"Really?" says Ernest, kissing his fiancée with a respectable fervor.

Some men will believe anything.

On the subject of male vanity, it might amuse you to know that at this very moment, Ellis Yuppington and his racquetball partner, Hubert Vondervender, are sauntering toward an Irish Juice Bar around the corner from the club. Ellis spots a young hooligan with a glue pot and a dozen *Careless Love* posters that he has been paid to plaster over the plywood at a construction site. Ellis and his racquetball partner stop to survey the hooligan's handiwork. Ellis feels a stirring in his manly groin.

"Kasha Varnishka. I hear they used someone else's body for the *Sports Illustrated* spread. They just glued on the head. Do it all the time. Airbrushing," remarks Vondervender.

Ellis isn't listening. He'd know that tongue anywhere. That's little Lizzie Edmunds wrapped in the arms of an extraterrestrial. "I can vouch for the other one. Used to go out with her. Nice kid. Maybe I'll give her a call."

Vondervender, who up until then has been somewhat unimpressed with Yuppington as a whole, makes mental note to transfer Ellis's number to his A list leather address book, in pen.

The elevator door opens. A photographer spots the loving couple and flash! Ernest and Lizzie blink for a full fifteen seconds before the green spots go away.

This is the beginning of celebrity.

Celebrity will certainly be a balm. But Lizzie could do so much better. Still, if it has to happen, I'd rather see her with Ernest than one of those West Coast impostors I've had so much trouble with. At least Ernest is sincere.

I am, however, happy that for the moment—and I do mean moment—she is happy.

She and Ernest decide that they will be married tomorrow morning.

I trust you are all familiar with the proverb, "Marry in haste, repent at leisure." Never, ever, no matter how swept up you are in the whirls and torrents, marry in haste unless you are dead certain that you are marrying me.

If you do, remember. Mistaken identity is grounds for annulment.

Marcy Contemplates the Purchase of a Vibrator

Marcy has seen them. Sometimes they are called neck massagers. They come in lifelike flesh tones and white. Sometimes they are sculpted to look like penises. If magazine articles and novels and sex manuals are to be believed these battery-operated gizmos are the wonder tool of the resourceful single gal. They all have one thing in common: To own one, you have to buy one. That involves either ordering one through the mail—and what is more telltale than the discreet brown wrapper with a P.O. box in the upper left-hand corner?—or walking up to a counter in a store that sells jiggling joysticks and saying, "I'd like one in beige, please. Nine inches. Yes, thank you. Circumcised would be fine. Do you take unmarked bills?"

Marcy considers either prospect so daunting that the pleasures of owning a vibrator may never be hers. She wonders what she's missing.

She's missing something that resembles a vibrator, but comes in a 190-pound carrying case complete with calorie-operated arms and legs. Something she doesn't mind being seen with.

It's been all right watching Dick on TV, but when the set's off, she's alone again. Marcy makes a decision. If she cannot bring herself to buy a vibrator, she absolutely has to reconnect with the male persuasion before her complexion goes to ruin.

In a blaze of determination, she dials Love at First Sight and boldly requests a date with the man of her champagne (Henriot, reserve Baron Philippe de Rothschild) wishes and caviar (Iron Gate Malossol Sevruga) dreams: Dick Judd.

Why didn't she think of this sooner? She did. Day and night. But she couldn't bear another disillusionment. Illusions were much more delish. And talk about safe sex.

For the next four days, Marcy goes on Dr. Mutanson's Double-Fudge Brownie diet. She wants to look her best. By Thursday, she has the shakes. After wantonly consuming a turkey sandwich, Marcy heads for Elizabeth Arden. Franzl does her face and a body wax. Friday, $3\frac{3}{4}$ pounds thinner, and without a trace of unwanted body hair, Marcy takes to her bed and recites her old mantra. It still works.

Dick

Marcy waits at the prime window table of Petruccio's outdoor café. To all that pass she gives the appearance of being a woman with considerable globe trottage under her Banana Republic webbed canvas belt. Her hair has been olive-oil conditioned and Luminized. To assure optimum lighting conditions, she applied her makeup an hour ago in Washington Square Park. Her Desert Blush lipstick is matte. Her eyes are awash with Visine. She drums her French manicured fingers, ten perfect white half-moons, on the marble tabletop as she taps her khaki leather Joan & David flats. She toys with the handle of her demitasse cup. The espresso is de-caf. She ordered it as a potential conversation starter. She actually can't drink anything but water without running the risk of discoloring her cinnamon-pink tongue.

From under the brim of her hat, she scans the passersby. She knows she's in the right place. Love at First Sight confirmed in writing. Marcy feels a little louche lounging in a Greenwich Village café. She might be mistaken for a well-to-do tourist, but she is willing to risk it.

Dick is flying in on his Lear for the rendezvous, and Petruccio's is his place of choice.

Marcy notices that she is not the only single person staring expectantly out the window. She begins to suspect that Petruccio's is owned by the folks at Love at First Sight. There can be no other explanation. And then, all of a sudden, it doesn't matter.

The earth stops turning. There he is. His hair falling across his brow; his loden coat open at the neck to show a ruby silk scarf. Marcy summons all her womanly powers to the task of appearing at ease. Through sheer will, her palms are warm and dry. She is more than ready.

Dick Judd checks the street sign, the awning over the restaurant. This is the right place. He boldly scrutinizes the faces in the window. He does not go unnoticed. He refers to a photograph he cradles in his hand. Marcy.

She pretends to be rummaging in her Fendi bag for her international date book. She finds it. Opens to a map of the Paris subway system. This gives Dick plenty of time to size up the situation. Then, after she's located the Louvre stop and counted *un, deux, trois,* she looks up and flashes her freshly cleaned and polished teeth. She raises her hand, fanning her fingers slightly.

Dick sees her. She sees him see her. He looks at her directly, then away.

Nope. Not at all what he had in mind. Marcy isn't the dynamic woman of the world destined to share his palatial lodge at Gstaad, his voice-activated sauna, the inherited snorkeling equipment used by Ernest Hemingway in the waters off Havana. Nope.

Dick doesn't bother to enter the café. Why go through the motions?

Marcy sees what she's seen every night on TV. She's dined with this man, told him things she's never told anyone else. And he's walking away, out of her life. There's a mistake. He needs glasses. Isn't that sweet? He really wears glasses but he wants to look his best for her. He obviously doesn't *see* her. There is only one thing to do.

"Dick!"

Dick keeps walking.

Marcy leaves five dollars on the table and grabs her coat. "Dick!"

Damned city noise. Who can hear anyone anymore anyway? Marcy jogs as quickly as she can without perspiring. Dick eludes her. Then he's gone altogether. Marcy stands on a street corner looking four ways.

No Dick. Her snapshot lies on the pavement, dusty with the Reebok prints of strangers.

Excuse me, my honey-lipped angel of joy, dearest one, something has come up.

It's a fever. Every color seems more brilliant against a pale gray sky. Oh, my beloved ones, are you angry with me? Do you curse me and ask yourselves, why I keep you waiting, how I can permit you to endure?

Love has no reason. I desire you above all others. Wait for me. I love you, I love you.

Pegasus whinnies and snorts. I haven't even a moment to saddle him. The sun splinters against my shining armor as I mount my rearing charger.

Marcy. Where is Marcy? She is in the corner store buying AA batteries and sunglasses. Oh, Marcy, don't waver. Don't ask directions to Dildorama. It's Time.

She hears the wind sweep past her ears. Fair Marcy, dearest damsel. Love is here.

She spots me. This time, there can be no mistake.

Marcy's hat falls to the sidewalk as I enfold her waist and whisk her away. She grasps Pegasus's golden mane as if she's always known how. We ride. Up and up. The air is thin. Marcy laughs. She doesn't look down or back.

But a word to you. Don't get any silly ideas.

Je t'embrasse. You know that. No tears, unless you just want to let some of those feelings out. Yes, my cherished one, I understand completely.

If, as I sweep Marcy away, you harbor doubts, set them to slumber a hundred years. Do you wonder how I can be all hers and all yours and faithfully devoted happily ever after to both of you separately all your lives? How I can be all things to all women, while being yours and yours alone?

Leave the niggling details to me.

With love, all things are possible.

Think of me and you will never be lonely. Let no man pull us asunder, though he may try. You will be put to many a test, my princess.

Remember, without you, I am nothing.

I remain, your,

P. Charming

XXOO

From the <u>New York Times</u> bestselling author
of <u>Morning Glory</u>

LaVyrle Spencer

One of today's best-loved authors
of bittersweet human drama and
captivating romance.

ALWAYS
AND
FOREVER

CYNTHIA
FREEMAN

A love story of extraordinary scope
and power, *Always and Forever* is
another gift of a writer who will be
long and lovingly remembered.

**Coming soon in hardcover
to bookstores everywhere.**

G. P. PUTNAM'S SONS